Solea Razvan

BALADA:
When my eyes
are weighed
with sleep I
quench the
evening
candle's
glow

When war rages across the
universe, which side are you
on?

Salonta
2015

Source of the cover art:

In the Center of the Trifid Nebula
Image Credit: Subaru Telescope (NAOJ), Hubble Space Telescope, Martin Pugh; *Processing:* Robert Gendler

http://apod.nasa.gov/apod/ap130128.html

Special Thanks to:

My sister Şolea Sabina for helping me with writer's block and to my parents Tania Carmen and Florin for supporting me.

ISBN: 978-973-0-18514-0.

Prologue.

'Nothing is impossible, just improbable.'

That's the concept that defines reality in any place and at any time.

This one starts in a realm that is beyond time and space, between existence and nothingness, far removed from heaven and hell, but at the same time it's as closest to those realms as such a thing is possible.

This place is not on any map, nor is there any way to make one, yet it is not a hidden realm.

It cannot be found if you look for it, but you enter and leave as often as once a day and traversing it is impossible with effort but comes natural with rest, and sometimes you remember it and sometimes you don't, but you where there, especially when you weren't.

This plane of existence has countless names, which have all been heard in an infinite number of languages, across innumerable galaxies and boundless universes.

This land is both beauty and ugliness combined, both salvation and damnation, but its description alone cannot be comprehended thoroughly in mere words, so let us stop here and let us name this place "the realm".

Here in 'the realm', its only inhabitants for this particular time and in this particular version are the 'Amurg' , ancient creatures whose place of origin has long been lost to the sands of time.

Amongst a gathering of various different 'Amurg', beings of all shapes, colors and sizes, who were gathered in a circle and playing a game of *cards*, a new one approached the group.

"Do any of you know where Deux is?" the Amurg asked the group.

"Oh, it's you! Ye Just got here didn't you?" *one of* the players turned from the game and looked at the newcomer…The first new Amurg in a long, long time to arrive at this realm. Initially his coming had caused a small stir in a realm that was usually ruled by monotony since its inhabitants were all immortal, but that soon died out and new question about the appearance of a new Amurg, or what were the consequences of his appearance were quickly forgotten so they could focus on more important matters.

Namely gambling.

"*Why* do you want to find Deux? The guy's a little weird, why don't you join the game, come here and relax." another one said and gestured for the newcomer to join the collective with what could be considered a friendly smile, at least to higher beings it was a friendly smile.

"*Gamble, waste time, that's all you do all day! How can you do that and not go insane from boredom is beyond my comprehension and since I have access to unlimited knowledge and wisdom that says a lot!*" The Amurg thought to himself angrily as he glared at the others.

"*I could tell you all what a disgrace you're actions are, how you waste your great potential, I could rant, rave or give calm compelling arguments, but.........Would you learn from them? Would you listen to them, would you understand my words........Would you even acknowledge them? No.....Because you don't care, nobody does, so in the end it doesn't matter.*" he added to his train of thoughts and once that was over he took a small breath of air to calm himself down.

"I just want to ask him a question, so does anyone know where he is?"

"He's sometimes west of here in the sandfields of a thousand nights, today's the day after the thousandth one, so you should be able find him there right about now." One of them replied.

The Amurg then turned to leave but was stopped by one last question.

"After you finish that, do you want to join the game?" Another one said to him with a degree enthusiasm that was mirrored by the other players.

"Does it matter if I join in?" he replied without turning back.

"*Of* course it does! T*he* game changes in so many *ways!*" Another one answered *and* went on to describe in great detail the many ways in which the game would change.

T*he* new comer then turned his head slightly back at the game, just enough so he could gaze at the players, at these creatures of immeasurable power and infinite potential who's most important activity and greatest desire was a card game. Words failed him as he once more felt anger at this waste of infinite potential, so the Amurg just tuned his head back in the direction he was going, leaving behind the confused all-powerful beings, who quickly got over it and continued with their g*a*me.

He walked towards the area where they said Deux would be with as much rigor as he could muster, spurred on by a subconscient defense mechanism that told him to leave the group as soon as possible, lest he too be infected by this 'disease' of laziness and the sheer lunacy of having the universe at your fingertips and only using those fingers to draw from a deck.

A*fter* a while he finally arrived at the sandfields and started looking around for his quarry.

"Trough the warp and from the shadows and barren desert fields.

Does a whisper come to be heard!"

"*Of* a tail of one hundred billion light years.

And a million galaxies' words!"

T*he* Amurg heard someone singing and looked around for the source.

"Hea*r* the tale of invincible strength that is born from a decade's long brew."

"And a thousand admirals who faced that force, but can never seem to break trough!"

"Hea*r* the tales of the great kings, queens and a hundred princes, who have the universe at their beck and call."

"But the one thing that their hearts desires, they will never have it at all!"

"Of ancient stories! Everlasting ballads!"

"Who change every time,

" Every verse; every rhyme,"

"When the story is told one more time!"

He looked to where the 'moonlight' of this realm shinned and from there he saw a shape that was flying down towards him, it was a floating two horse carriage that was filled with merchandise and it was its driver was the one that was singing.

"So come with me now, to the place beyond mirrors and light!"

"Where hidden secrets are in plain view for the worthy to find;"

"To where? I do not know, so come and see the things hidden in plain sight!"

"To long forgotten realms, that appears when you open your mind!"

"See a place which is more uncanny than what you imagined could be;"

"From the deep dreamland, to the heaven's endless sky!"

"As what's real is stranger than any fiction I you could see."

"As the truth is more unbelievable than a lie!"

The carriage finally descended before him and its driver looked at the Amurg with glee in its eyes.

"Are you Deux?" he asked the figure made out of black mist and white flesh, with eyes that did not blink who was sitting in the driver's seat, his shape and form was forever changing, with the only thing that remained constant was his three pairs of eyes and his strange hands that had claws which seemed like they were not made to tear flesh.

"Oh it's you, you came much earlier than I expected!" Deux said to him with an eerily cheerful voice as he gazed at the new Amurg which had a humanoid appearance, was dressed in what appeared to be a long flowing robe, with a square cap on his head with a piece of cloth streaming down one side, but the most distinct thing about him was the fact that when you looked at his face, not matter how hard you tried you could not see any distinguishable facial features, he could have been anybody and yet he appeared to be nobody.

"What do you mean by that?"

"You don't remember do you?" Deux asked him.

"Remember what?"

"What you were before you became an Amurg of course!"

"Of course I don't! You've been here longer than me and you haven't even learned that by now!?" the new comer replied.

Upon hearing the second half of the sentence a great smile appeared on his faces.

"Sorry, just asking, so why are you here?"

"I'm here to ask if you are Deux."

"And if I am what of it?"

"I heard that Deux was bored of this realm and went on a journey to visit the other realms, I want to do the same, but since there are so many I want to hear your story, so that I may know which one is the most fun of them all, after spending who knows how much time in this cesspool of boredom I need that! So will you tell me about your journey?" The Amurg replied.

"So you want me to tell you my story, ey? Why I have lots of stories! For example the story of this great blade! Why this is the blade of the one who faced a billion foes and fought a thousand battles and won all of them! Well one of his many weapons actually."

"That looks like a field plow and a cheap one made from different scraps cobbled together!"

"I know sir! You want only the best and I the greatest merchant of all have it! For example this is the secret weapon of the greatest spy that has ever lived!" Deux said and handed him the aforementioned object to examine.

"Twenty two gardenias from Halina's flower emporium, one dinner reservation with at the Rotzwenen, one new camera.' this looks like some secretaries to do book! What possible use could a spymaster have for this as a tool for espionage warfare? Reschedule them to death!?"

"I know sir! And as such I feel obliged to hand you our greatest item yet! Why, within this jar is the means with which half a universe was united and the other half conquered!"

"That, my friend is a jar filled with sand!" the Amurg paused to let that statement sink in.

"Are you actually trying to sell me sand, here in a desert!" the statement was so 'unique' that the one who said it had trouble believing that he actually said such words.

"I see your right again sir, enough with the cheap stuff! Let's get to the high caliber merchandise! As such I have-"

"Forget this! If you're not going to tell me of your journey them I'm goin-"

"-the journal in which I wrote down my travels." Deux said and the Amurg paused mid turn and returned his gaze to Deux.

"Why didn't you say that in the first place?!"

"Well, I got to make a living don't I?"

"You're an immortal creature who doesn't need to eat and can make anything from nothing by merely thinking about it! What possible need would you have for an income?!"

"About the same reason another immortal creature would seek out a traveler's stories, when he could just use his powers to see the 'spoilers' himself." Deux said with a wide grin as the other Amurg remained silent for a moment.

"How do I know it's not another piece of junk, like what you showed me before?"

"Why don't I read it to you and if you like it you can buy it, after all a good story is worth reading over and over again wouldn't you agree?"

"All right, let's get started." the Amurg said trying to sound bored and annoyed, but you could detect eagerness in his voice and to that Deux grinned even more, since it was obvious he had hooked a customer.

"Though I must warn you it is a long story, and it will take a while for me to tell all of it."

"We're immortals you idiot!" the Amurg shouted towards Deux in a fit of frustration.

"Alright, aright! Yeeesh, you think with everlasting life you wouldn't be in such a rush!" Deux said to him as he exited the carriage and sat down, he then brought out his journal and reading glasses, took from behind his back a picnic basket and set it down between himself and the Amurg.

He then held the book at an angle that did not allow the Amurg to see the writing on the pages; Deux cleared his voice for a few moments before opening the book.

"Why do you need all of this stuff for?" The Amurg asked him.

"Atmosphere of course, if I'm going to tell a story I must look the part, let me read you from my own writings. Now where to begin? " he thought for a while before deciding on one particular story that he enjoyed and started reading it with a smile.

"In one of the many realms of existence, long ago in a galaxy that was once far away but now is close, that although similar to others, it still differed from them greatly!"

"For in this particular galaxy sentient beings had conquered the stars, but instead of using technology as their main tool another one was chosen. Here what powered their space fleets, orbiting stations and gave them strength was magic!"

"This is the story of the end of an era and the beginning of a new one, of those who lived it, those who died during it and those who brought about this new age, of those who did great things, some good, some evil, but great things nonetheless!" Deux read towards the Amurg who for the first time since arriving in this realm he felt happy and if he could he would have smiled.

"Finally something that matters!" he thought to himself as the story started.

When my eyes are weighed with sleep I quench the evening candle's glow

Excerpt, from the works of Grand Scholar, and The Great War Expert Djanus Todomari from the Imperium Archives

On Caliupus 27th, Imperial year 1898, Federal year 3941, and Republican year 953 on the small home world of the Tolstoy sector, a Federal fleet clashed for less than 3 hours with an Imperial one. This small battle which was the first shot in The Great War was situated above a place called Graperust Manor, owned by a Novo Albetan lawyer called William Murasaki Kuckluck.

After the Battle of Graperust, mister Murasaki said that he had enough of the whole affair and decided to move his family 560.000 light-years to a town called New Hope within the Tremera system, to a house called Woodgrom Courthouse with the intention of avoiding the war in its entirety.

Years later the commanders of the belligerent forces came to that very same courthouse to sign the ending of all hostilities. So when it was over Mr Murasaki could boast that the war began on his front lawn porch and ended in his backyard gazebo.

The Great War raged across millions of star systems, billions of planets and trillions of light years, within it farm workers from Nova Bronze City of the Towar System, clashed with fisherman from Seshrim 9, lawyers and schoolteachers from the Brumbaki Plains of Bulla 8 with doctors and accountants from The Tjigu asteroid cluster.

Whole nations and ways of life would disappear only to be replaced by new ones and within this age of chaos great heroes and villains would emerge, several sentients would join the war, each from the three superpowers, they would be at the most crucial and most bloody of the battles and somehow survive them all, and give testimony of just how unrealistic reality could become.

A smuggler would save a country , a shadow warrior would emerge from the darkness, a rebel would reshape the galaxy, a sentient would change the way things were forever, and a potions brewer who did not go a single day to military school would become the greatest commander the known universe had ever seen or perhaps would ever see. So the sands of time flowed and with their passing the universe changed forevermore.

Grand Scholar and Great War Expert Djanus Todomari

Imperium Archives

Within the warp.

9:52 Imperial Fleet Time

A great train traversed the thin plane of hyperspace, it was a massive construct composed of at least 2.000 individual wagons, each one of them was over a hundred meters in diameter and stretched for at least five times that, but despite the titanic nature of this interstellar vehicle by the standards of its kind it was the runt of the litter.

These wagons where forged out of fine tempered steel with a smooth surface and each wagon's front and back ended with a conic shape head and tail.

Seven great horizontal sheets of metal extended across their bodies, starting at the front and ending at the rear of each wagon, runes which glowed bright with energy where embedded on these stripes and from them magical energy was released for the purpose of moving and guiding the train towards its destination.

These bursts of energy started as a single line, that at certain points of its length bent upwards, downwards, left and right, and at each bent smaller lines formed from them, which they themselves bent and made new ones emerge, giving the magic the shape of a great tree branch that looked like it sprouted from lighting itself.

But it was only the shape of a plant and nothing more, for the purpose of this train was not the production of breathable air or that of fruits or flowers.

No, its purpose was transportation and among its cargo where two very important passengers.

A surge of energy, which was called since ancient times a gust of warp wind shook the space train, not enough to cause any damage or deviate it from its course, but enough to wake up one of the occupants of its VIP room from his nap.

For a few brief moments confusion and disorientation dominated his person, that was generally what happened when you traverse the realm of reality and the realm of dreams and no more so than when you are inside the warp which existed outside both of them.

For it was a very mysterious and unnerving place and even veteran sailors and soldiers where not to comfortable with passing through this plane which seemed to be nowhere yet everywhere at the same time.

As for the drivers of this train the feeling of dread caused by venturing in a place outside of what you considered your 'normal reality' was present to them as well. Even though they've learned to overcome it and even partially control it, its presence remained an eerie reminder that they didn't belong here.

So you should now be able to understand the temporary confusion of the aforementioned passenger, but that quickly gave away to remembrance, as he now reacquainted himself with this plane of existence and thus the confusion disappeared as his mind recovered from the daze and remembered everything and realized that he was on a galactic train, souring in the limitless heavens of space towards its stop.

It was an Imperial Fleet supply train, carrying essential food, medicine, clothing, and ammunition for the 378th Corps that was stationed on planet Volun 4. The train slithered its way through the warp like some great celestial dragon towards its destination with those supplies, along with the aforementioned corps's new commander and his knight and chief of staff.

Namely the newly minted Commodore First Class Metternich per Pelasgiamus and his knight Commodore third class Adrian de Morowetz.

Metternich was a unique creature amongst the Empire, his hair was black as night and shortly trimmed, but not in a military stile, more like a summer style.

His skin was dark blue, which was not unheard of in the Empire but not entirely common and finally his eyes where perhaps the most unique thing about him, for their retina was a blue one, but his sclera was of a bright glowing red, which combined with his skin and his voice which was low and a bit gruff made him a very imposing visual figure.

His uniform consisted of black leather boots, black pants that were secured to his waist by a belt, along with as sheathed sword on his left side, a dagger on the back side of his belt, and a one handed crossbow on his right, his chest was covered in a black tunic, on his shoulder pads where three golden bars that symbolized his rank of Commodore First Class.

On his chest where it curbed to his sides was two lines of gold buttons united by a series of golden ropes that traversed his chest, they where for both decorative and practical purposes, since the real buttons where on the inner side of the left flap of the tunic.

He looked like someone who was born for war, who belonged on the battlefield, who would stand when others would fall, that was something no one could deny! Too bad he was a coward.

"Did you sleep well my liege?" Adrian asked him, he was dressed in the exact same uniform as Metternich but there was one bar on each shoulder to display his rank of Third Class.

Adrian was an Avian, his race was humanoid in its appearance, he had white feathers encompassing his entire skin, a great golden beak for a mouth and two black eyes that looked like they were constantly zoning into space, also his aforementioned feathers where ruffled and his beak had a slight dent in it, giving poor Adrian the appearance more aching to a crazed half dead chicken than that of a professional soldier. But he was anything but weak, as his past foes or rather the absence of past foes, or any foes for that matter was a very good testament to his skill.

"About as well as one can, given the current circumstances." Metternich replied and Adrian gave a nod of agreement and said nothing else, he too felt uncomfortable traveling through hyperspace, but he was more unnerved by being on a train instead of a ship than the fact that he was in the warp.

"I've been meaning to ask Adrian, why when we are about to meet new people do you always stop grooming yourself?" Metternich enquired.

"People don't take you seriously when they first meet you if you don't look pretty, their true nature comes out easier that way, good thing wouldn't you say?" Adrian asked and gave a slight smile to his commander, one which Metternich returned in kind.

Ever since they first met, Metternich had always treated him with the upmost respect and professionalism you'd come to expect an officer of his rank to give and receive, that had made an impression on Adrian, which was what eventually convinced him to become Metternich's follower, a fact that the Commodore would be secretly grateful for but also secretly resentful for the rest of his life, but generally more times he would be the former rather than the latter.

The seconds ticked away in silence and seeing that the conversation had died down for the moment, Metternich decided to once more go over the briefing papers he had been given for his new command.

He was using a farview screen to review them and after that was done he started to once more research the culture of the opposing nation.

The farview or rather this variant of it, was a rectangular shaped mass of crystals with magic runes embedded on its surface, that when activated a mist like gas would emerge from its screen and take the shape and color of whatever the farview's user desired, or if he preferred it could only project 2d images on its surface, it was very flexible device!

It was also a very useful tool, one which Metternich regularly used since he could have hundreds or thousands of books stored on it, making it easier to carry and ideal for alleviating boredom.

But as they got closer and closer to their destination, he silently wished for eternal boredom.

"I'll take a lifetime of boredom over any war or battle, at least boredom doesn't come running towards you with a big sharp magical weapon with the intent to play squash with your head!" he thought to himself, hoping that this tranquility would last forever, but like all good things it had to eventually come to an end, for a beeping sound was heard from the ships internal speakers signaling that they were getting near the exit of the warp and that soon they would be arriving at they're destination.

"It is a good thing that they decided to use a warp portal train instead of a ship to get us there, last thing we need is some bloody raid ambushing us before we arrive at our new command." Adrian said to his liege.

"Well, despite the best attempts of the seemingly universal and unstoppable power of stupidly to make a wrong decision, the vile forces of logic and reasoning have seemingly prevailed and vanquished this oh, so great foe!" Metternich said in a hammy tone which clearly indicated he was joking and Adrian showed his appreciation with a good chuckle.

A warp portal was as its name suggests, a portal that is situated on a planet or in outer space which allows faster travel trough the warp if a ship is not using a portal, making it at least twice as fast if not more depending on the state of the warp between two points, the size of the gate and the amount of power it had access too.

Also, when in hyperspace there was the danger of being ripped apart by gravity fields or energy nexuses if a ship was not in peak condition or low on power and if it was traversing a less than ideal hyperspace route, well you get the general idea.

Why a wandering comet, a small dust field, of even the remains of a small passing solar flare could tear a ship apart!

A warp portal along with the great power provided by either the sun or a planet's energy nexus engulfed a ship or in this case a train in a protective field as it traversed the warp, protecting it to a certain degree from such perils and shredding whatever was in its way, as long as it was not too great an obstacle.

Also ships who did not use jump gates had to have a build in warp sanctuary and plenty of power crystals to make the jump, a ship using a jump gate would not require an expensive warp sanctuary or power storage crystals in order to jump, all the ship needed was it to be was airtight, also the energy required to enter and exit the warp was provided by the starting gate and the destination gate, thus the gates where faster and cheaper and that was always the way to go.

But for all its advantages the aforementioned warp train had no means of its own to enter and exit warp without a gate.

It was also impossible for trains to change and adjust their route when using one, this was one area where they where outclassed by ships.

Also if you're enemies manage to find just the right conditions along you're potential route with the train, they could pull you out of the warp and ambush you, a train of course could be retrieved with a special support ship designed just for that purpose and be back on its way, but until then it was vulnerable to attack.

But that was a moot point since military trains where armed to the teeth, that combined with their long bodies gave them excellent options for defense, they could form a protective sphere or dodecahedron, which unlike ships had no vulnerable point and had excellent anti-light ships defenses, it truly was the safest way to travel when confronted with pirates or enemy space raiders.

Fully fledged warships where an entirely different matter and when it came to that a ship was the way to go if you wanted to outmaneuver and outrun them.

So it was a constant debate between the advantages of rigidness but high security against greater flexibility with freedom but also the presence of an unknown danger and many supporters of both sides argued day and night over which was best.

For both means of transportation had their pros and cons, but for the current route which took the train trough friendly territory and lands in which the Empire was the dominant power (at least for now) the train was best suited for such a purpose, also many would think that a fleet corps commander would never 'lower' himself to ride a simple train instead of a battleship and that was also the reason Metty chose this, since it also gave him the element of surprise over his potential enemies.

And for the young Commodore First Class that thought brought him some piece of mind from his troubles.

"Though I am grateful that I will not have to worry about being torn to shreds by some small space pebble or flying into a mine field and being ambushed while traversing or entering a new system, the idea that I have to face death sooner rather than latter is not a very appealing one."

Metternich thought to himself as he lamented the sad state of affairs he currently found himself in and within his mind he briefly looked back on how he had arrived to his current predicament, thoughts that he would eventually write down in his posthumous memoirs.

Extract from the book "Confessions, an Admirals tale volume I"

For the past three years I had been a sailor in the Imperial navy, since that was what the state wanted of its citizens whether they were willing or not and despite my titanic efforts to avoid the whole war, fate had other plans for me!

Before the war I was running a medical transport business and one day my ship was boarded by a pirate raiding party from the Republic and like any sane sentient with half a brain I immediately surrendered and asked for parole, which was a fancy way of saying: 'If I do not fight you and surrender all my goods, you will do me the honor of not introducing my brain to your axe'.

It worked out for the most part, the aforementioned Republicans seemed alright ,about as alright as killers and thieves and God knows what other kind of madmen and women from one of the most savage dictatorship know to the galaxy could be.

It was only myself and Akanthos that day and I am grateful for the fact that none of the women who sometimes served on my ship where present.

Thrust me, those Republicans may look like pleasant fellows, with they're silky long hair, pointy ears, shiny skin, and deep beautiful eyes and absolutely gorgeous humanoid anatomy(just because I don't like them, doesn't mean I can't admit they're pretty!) but that's the only good thing about them.

Though I am not saying that their particular brand of savagery was worst that the one practiced by the Empire or Federation oh no, we all had an equal timeshare in that, theirs was just of a different flavor, that's all.

And to be hones as individuals they were pretty decent fellows.

That is if you're not they're rivals, of which the Imperium or Empire as it was called back then (and is still used in battle cries) found itself at that particular moment in time.

As they looted our ship taking anything they could: pills, syrup, cushions, fabric and fabric samples for footstools (seriously what kind of pirates steals stool samples?) at one point they opened the crates that contained bottles filled with medicinal alcohol.

Alcohol that was to be specifically used externally and only externally!

And pirates being pirates they immediately opened the bottles and started drinking it, granted the alcohol was put into recycled wine bottles, but unlike what the press would want you to believe, we did not intentionally put them in those bottles in the faint hope that pirates would pop out of nowhere and start consuming them, but rather the fact that the bottles were cheap, at the ready and reliable for our purposes and since our venture was a small one we needed every penny we could skim!

So I tried frantically to warn them, because honestly who deserves a slow and painful death? But my pleas fell on deaf ears, mostly from the fact that they did not speak Imperial Standard and I was not familiar with their language, that and the fact that at that point in time the two of us where both tied and gagged in a corner of the room, made my chivalrous intentions doomed to failure.

Well not a total failure, the by then half drunken pirates where having a good laugh at how the two of us where moaning and struggling with the ropes and gags as we tried to stop them and one of our viewers liked out impromptu mime show so much that he decided to reward me with a good kick in the chest that made me collapse to the ground and elicit a bout of laughter from his comrades.

A moment later the rest of our adoring audience joined in to let me know just how much they 'appreciated' me and they appreciated me a lot!

It only lasted a few moments but it was like hell, but even so I wanted to stop them from consuming the alcohol.

And to those of you who did not spent their youth studying medicine, the reason medicinal alcohol is not used for consumption is that there is the danger of it containing methanol, which is a very poisonous type of alcohol, why just 10 ml of the stuff can render you permanently blind and 30 ml can kill you!

Now don't misunderstand, every bottle of medicinal alcohol is purified before being released to the general public, but the main problem with our stock was that we where transporting it to a purifying facility! And with those idiots chugging it down their throats like it was ice tea on a beach you can guess what followed immediately after.

Now, I was not to fond of them back then and my opinion over the years has not changed by much, but even if they where a cutthroat band of thieves and murderers, who if they could they would have sold both me and Akanthos to be some plantation owner's slaves or worst playthings, but as I said before a slow and painful death in which you become blind, you're insides burned, every muscle in your body spasmed and intense pain jolted throughout your body was not something I would wish on anyone, not even them!

So I laid there on the floor waiting for the inevitable and when it came it was truly horrible, a great scream of agony erupted from every pirate, forming a hellish choir that could be heard from all over the ship, as one by one the poor souls had their fates sealed.

As the grotesque scene unfolded around me, a sudden flash of light and a great boom came from my left, I turned my head to see what had just happened. Much to my horror, I discovered that one of the pirates in his pain induced frenzy had fired an arrow into one of his comrades, incinerating the poor or fortunate taffer in an instant.

This made all hell break loose or rather more of it, as the pirates started firing their bows and swinging their sword and maces around causing an inferno of fire, water, ice, wind, earth to engulf the corridors, of my ship and the pirate's ship.

Akanthos managed to get hold of a broken bottle and cut his bonds free and bless his souls he dragged my beaten and bloodied body to the sleeping quarters, where we locked the doors and waited for the carnage to end.

After a few minutes of what can only be describe as a wall of horrid sounds, silence fell and after untying me and waiting what seemed like an eternity, we armed ourselves with the axes that our ship had in case of fire outbreaks, opened the doors and cautiously peered out to have a look.

What we saw was something out off a horror movie, bodies laid everywhere, blood, excrement, and piss pouring out from them, the walls where filled with scars from the weapons discharge and a foul smell of death permeated the entire hull.

We continued our little journey throughout the ship, driven by a curiosity, which when you stop to think about it was borderline suicidal, but to our luck every pirate had consumed the alcohol.

After a few minutes we located the captain of this pirate crew and after a few gentle prods from my axe, we could finally relax.

I thought that the worst was over and gave out a breath of relief, when all of a sudden the ship shook violently. Akanthos and myself gave each other a look of worry, we both hoped that the warp sanctuary had not been damaged, when all of a sudden the sound of footsteps echoed throughout the ship as the door before us was blasted open and armed warrior poured in.

Much to our relief it was the Imperial Fleet who had boarded our vessel, the cavalry had arrived! A little late for my taste, but that's big government for you!

And I must say the look on their faces was priceless, behind me there was a corridor filled with battle scars, dead pirates all about and there I was bruised and bloodied, standing atop of the pirate captain with a bloody axe in hand(courtesy of my prodding of the corpse a moment ago to ensure that he had expired).

At that moment I felt like I was on cloud nine, but unfortunately for me, news of that incident spread far and wide, word of Captain Metternich who single handedly killed 50 pirates with his bare hands became the talk of the local subsector.

After that a bunch of reporters came to cover the story and Akanthos being the sly business man that he was, charged them heavily for each interview, thus things where looking bright for us!

We had gotten out of a tight spot alive, we now had a very healthy sum of money to help our business expand and we were small town heroes in our neck of the woods (something the ladies appreciated) it was a small piece of heaven, but regretfully it did not last.

For a certain Commodore James Crackerjack had heard of our little adventure and the brainless glory hound immediately showed up a few days later and demanded I transfer to his command, the fact that I was a civilian and my trade was 'potions making' which by law protected me from drafting since I *worked in healthcare was completely ignored by the tosser and despite my best efforts to get into his thick skull, the idiot ignored logic and reasoning and continued to press the issue.*

Under normal circumstances I would have walked away, but remember that he was not some regular loony but a loony with a license to kill from the state, that and old James was not only a fool, he was a fool with a fleet of a hundred warships behind him and so much to my horror, they gave me my uniform, slapped a couple of golden buttons on my collar to show that I was now officially a Captain and thus I was dragged into the fleet.

Akanthos was ignored in all of this, that much was owned to the fact that sentients tend to only acknowledge the apparent leader of a group when that group allegedly does something impressive, so I somehow managed to convince Old Mad Jack to let him go on the grounds that he was my underling and he had to make sure my businesses' where looked after, him being an aristocrat and having some semblance of a brain nodded and let it be so and I was glad for that, I mean no sense in both of us going to hell I suppose.

So that's how I found myself being torn from a safe place, a newly minted Captain, given a ship which I christened 'The Vampire's Vengeance', with a crew that consisted at the top of the following: first officer Lieutenant James 'Butcher' Centengu, Logistics officer Sergeant Alega 'Baker' Sovorovda, and finally science and engineering officer Lieutenant Lloyd Colomas 'Candlestickmaker' Firebark and with this we were sent to fight in various mini wars and full blown wars over the years leading up to the Great War.

And that my readers, is how my inglorious career began, with poisoned drinks, crazy luck, a lot of pain, and my personal favorite stupidity and the eternal question of why such a combination exists and what it has against good and honest folk and me of course.

Metternich per Pelasgiamus, Freelance Potions Maker

"Nuts!" Metternich muttered under his breath as his mind stopped its wondering and returned to the present.

And with the memories of how he had arrived at his current predicament still fresh in his mind, he for a few minutes entered into a slight depression, which was comparable to that of a canary who upon being captured in the jaws of a cat became impatient and said to the aforementioned feline: 'just do it already!' with indifference to its fate.

He thought of his current situation.

On the one hand having a few hundred ships and several thousands of warriors to stand behind when the warp cannons, missiles and energy beams started flying was a good thing, on the other he also had to worry about even more enemy soldiers targeting him, so a mixed blessing at best!

After his first battle and the first sight of his dead soldiers he had tried to think of his subordinates as nothing but tools, tried to distance himself from them, hoping to ease his guilt when they would eventually die in future battles, but it did not work and no matter how many victories he achieved and despite knowing that he couldn't have done anything better in the past to avoid his subordinates dying, he still wondered if he could have saved them.

Maybe if he had been faster, stronger or smarter he could have prevented more of his soldiers from dying, but that was not possible and even now, years after he was drafted he could still remember just how many had died, what their last moments where, but what really weight heavily on his mind was the fact that he was starting to forget their names and they're faces where starting to slip from his mind.

He knows that before he manages to leave the fleet, he will have forgotten even more names and faces and that would haunt him forever, making him contemplate the 'easy' way out.

After a few minutes Metternich banished those vile thoughts, since in his opinion life was always worth living and you had to do your best to get over you're more difficult moments and move on.

That and the prospect of being turned into a corpse if he didn't snap out of it and get his act together or the prospect of eternal hellfire for choosing the 'easy way' made him come to his senses.

Releasing out a breath of mental exhaustion, he placed the farview he was using to research the culture of the Volunians on the table and laid back and relaxed for a few minutes.

"A sad state of affairs this is Lord Metternich, this corps has a lot of good warriors and officers, properly deployed it is deadly, yet it is being misused in a tertiary role in the war against Volunia!" Adrian lamented to his master as he took out a small box from his pocket, extracted a pill from it and swallowed the pill, breaking Metternich's state of mind with a not unwelcomed distraction from his less than cheerful thoughts.

"Don't linger too much on feelings of regret, think positive thoughts or you run the risk or seeing even the good side of life as meaningless." he replied.

"Yes sir, but I'm still a little depressed at this state of affairs." Adrian replied.

"Don't be, I'm rather pleased myself!" Metternich said to his knight.

"My lord?" Adrian replied as he turned his head towards his liege, his head filled with confusion.

"Why do you think I accepted this commission?"

"For the challenge?" Adrian said to his commander with a smile on his face, one that grew bigger once Metternich gave a nod of the head as his reply.

"But what I really meant to say is that here there is little chance of us being slaughtered by elite units from the enemy, thus we may be able to spent the whole war without the danger of us getting killed, but that's just my opinion, it only applies to me and I doubt it matters much to others." Metternich thought to himself. He then looked at Adrian and started to wonder if his knight did not have certain problems, since Adrian always showed great doubt one moment and great resolve the next and despite not being an expert on the behavior of Adrian's species, he wondered if not perhaps he was also wearing a mask and knowing a thing or two about living a lie, he could understand if sometimes you let the mask slip, but that was a train of thought for another time, especially since the warp train was reaching its destination.

Just then his communication crystal started vibrating, indicating that someone wanted to talk to him.

He touched the crystal with his finger and it morphed into the small shape of a serpentine creature with grey scales, who was dressed in the same manor of uniform as the two had, but instead of the tricorn caps which he and Adrian wore, this serpentine creature wore a side cap that made it clear he was a staff officer and not a command one. His uniform stretched from his neck down to the end of his body, engulfing him entirely in the dark material, the sailor belonged to the Balfarmaini, sentients who where a serpent like race that had no arms or legs , but they made due with a very powerful telekinetic ability which allowed them to levitate and use objects close to their bodies, this ability was very handy to the aforementioned Metty, since this was Lieutenant Butz his personal aide who had been with him for almost as long as Adrian had been, and served as his assistant, driver, bodyguard, and whatever other role was needed, that was pointed out by the fact that Butz's body was covered in all kinds of pouches filled with everything from food, to drink, to medicine and all kinds of objects and tools, anything that Metternich might need.

"My lord, the train has reached the base." Butz said to his commander.

"Thank you Butz." Metternich said as he touched the farview at a certain point which started it's deactivation process, but not before putting a bookmark on where he had left off, namely on the painting named *"Fate"*.

"Time to go Adrian! You said that this unit contains a lot of gifted officers?" he said to Adrian as he hesitated for a few moments, the option of delaying for a while was still open to him, especially since technically his new command wouldn't be official until he arrived, but after a moment of deliberation, he closed his farview, sealed it with string and they walked towards the train's exit. After all, the inevitable could only be put off for so long.

"Yes my lord, the corps's commanders where all upper and lower classmates of mine at the academy and I can vouch for their skills. They are the finest soldiers in the Empire!" Adrian proudly said to his liege.

"Then why have they been sent here to a dumping ground unit? Metternich asked him.

"I have already told you the reason for that sire." Adrian replied with regret and disappointment in his voice.

"Smart officers being sent away so those who are higher in rank but less in skill will not be outshined."

Metternich thought to himself and despite feeling a small sensation of joy, since it meant that it was even less likely that this would become the main theater of operations, but still he did lament the sad state of affairs the Empire seemed to be in since the beginning of its existence or at least since he arrived.

" No matter how many or how bright the stars are, they pale when compared to the Sun, so the stars make sure no one sees the glory of the Sun.'" he quoted an ancient war poem to his knight.

"Yes Excellency, but 'no matter how long or endless the starry night is, it always surrenders to the sun's morning light'." Adrian replied to his liege and looked at him with a proud smile and near hero worship in his eyes.

"You know you don't have to call me that, technically you've got better blood, pedigree, fortune and social rank than me; Hell! Up until three standard years ago I would be the one calling you my lord or something like that." Metternich said to him.

"That is one of the few positives of war my lord, injustices like what you said earlier are rectified as great leaders rise to take their rightful place in society!" he replied.

"I consider myself a lucky man and an intelligent one rather than someone who has been blessed by heaven to be a leader Adrian."

"That may be sir, but even then there are few people with those attributes and even fewer that occupy positions of authority and now the Empire needs them more than ever, which is why I believe you're one who is destined for great things!" Adrian said and before Metternich could reply he added the following:

"The Great Founder of our Empire also said that she was lucky."

At this Metternich half opened his mouth to counter but decided against it, Adrian was the type who was not only stubborn to a degree , but also very smart as well and by doing a quick onceover of the conversation he realized that he had just inadvertently quoted the Great Founder and his attempt to deflate his image had been interpreted by Adrian as humility, something that people like Adrian took it as something that reinforced the image of the great heroes handpicked by the Force of Creation to lead the Empire to greatness.

So the Commodore only inhaled a deep breath of air and tried to enjoy what few peaceful moments he had left before arriving at the boarding ramp.

"I may as well quit while I'm ahead, I'll be needing every ounce of wit I posses in order to find a way to somehow survive here at the very edge of the civilized galaxy." Metternich thought to himself as the ramp's door opened and he crossed the point of no return.

Excerpt from the diary of Private Raz V'a van;

from the book

"We were the legionaries of Malus 'The World Breaker'"

"It was my second month of dessert warfare on Volun 4 and up until now our only enemy was boredom since for the past 5 weeks there had been no activity along the front and I was enjoining a pleasant breakfast while listening to the morning music and the local weather news broadcast.

Are you cold tonight?

Do you worry tonight?

Are you sad tonight?

Well tomorrow will come,

With the first rays of sun,

And tonight will be here no more.

"A lovely song, and now for the latest development for the upcoming storms. An unpredicted change is about to occur within four locations, those situated in mountainous regions may expect a strong blow, to come from the southern direction, the city folk can this time rest at ease, with the exception of the local capitals, which are expected have its first share of heavy fall in what appears to be an unpredictable pattern. Those of you who have decided to take a long walk into virgin territory I hope you are prepared for the coming storm and finally chaotic fog is expected to befall on the western parts, mainly beaches and vacation areas and for the coming seasons the storm is believed to produce great change in the environment and medium.......but we would like to assure our listeners, that no matter how hard the storm hits..... it may seem dreadful and without end, but like all things good and bad it will eventually come to pass......"

We will be warm,

And safe from the storm,

And tonight will be here no more!

The sparrows will soar,

With the light from the shore.

And tonight will be here no more!

The windwaker, which some clever bastard had hooked up to a coin machine to charge us a penny a minute told us the latest news or at least it did after I placed a coin in its mouth.

But the peace was not to last, for we had received word that we would have a new commander, namely Commodore Metternich per Pelasgiamus. The news was greeted with mixed results among our ranks the majority received it well since the young Commodore was a Hero of the Empire and had made quite the name for himself, for he and his ship 'The Vampire's Vengeance' were renowned for their struggle against our Empire's enemies.

'Headmaster Metty is here!', 'The Fox of Marengo has arrived!', where the joyous cries of many sailors and soldiers.

Others were indifferent and some reacted with distain since a new commander meant things would change and if it was one thing being the army taught us it was that you can be sure that a soldier's world would be bad, go to hell and then things would start to get nasty.

Those were the thoughts going through my mind as I was walking to where our company's doctor was staying in order to get some Drava pills, which was medicine that gave you extra energy to stay awake and some extra stamina for fighting, the side effect was that it blocked any kind of dreams you could have while you were asleep.

That may have been a good thing since from that day on things would go from bad to worse and beyond, for what we would see in the upcoming battles would have only given us nightmares.

Private Raz V'a van, Imperial Logistic and Engineer Corps.

The Occupied Territories, planet Maramanakama, the Capital city Tolina, the Dukhym district.

9:53 Local Planetary Time.

Explosions raged as fire, wind, water and earth attacks of the city's resistance cell ambushed the local Imperial patrol or rather they had done a reasonable first volley against them, for after the element of surprise wore off, the Imperial units quickly got over their initial confusion and counterattacked.

First by raising they're shields and immediately activating the earth spells within them, drawing the ground around them to form a protective wall to block any more attacks and then launching a volley of their own against the interlopers, in that instance the battle changed from a seemingly successful ambush to a slaughter of the members of this group of Maran resistance fighters as they slowly but surely started falling to the might of the Empire.

A great explosion shook and reshaped the rooftop where Ahmaianos along with his fellow rebel fighters where, making him loose consciousness from the explosion, but after a moment of pitch darkness he opened his eyes to his new surroundings.

Ahmaianos the leader of the local resistance cell gave the order to pull back, and retreated behind the edge of the building's rooftop to avoid enemy fire, he looked to his left and right and realized that he was the last survivor of his squad. The others had all fallen or rather had been burned, crushed or sliced apart by the enemy's attacks, leaving nothing but body parts rather than bodies behind.

Upon this realization, anger filled him at seeing his friends' death, so he retreated even farther from the edge of the rooftop and jumped across to the neighboring buildings and continued his journey across rooftops until he managed to flank the enemy from behind.

 From there he peered over the edge to look at the Imperials who were still firing at where his squad had fallen.

 He aimed an arrow with his crossbow at one of the attackers and fired the weapon at the soldier that seemed to be the commander, the small arrow gathered the water vapors from the atmosphere and turned it into a small vortex of ice around its body, the arrow did not penetrate his armor, but the force of the impact and the cold air from the arrow got into his lungs freezing them, making him collapse to the ground.

 The squad seeing their commander go down immediately looked to were the shot was fired and quickly retaliated in kind with their own arrows.

Ahmaianos ducked and ran from the rooftop he was on and down a fire escape, as he looked back he saw how the fire arrows burned the roof, how the wind arrows blew around it and intensified the fire, and how the earth arrows absorbed matter from the surrounding buildings and grew many times their size, smashing anything that was in their way.

"They're so many…….and so powerful…….." he said to himself between gasps for air as he continued his desperate jog for life and limb; when he found himself on ground level and in one of the back alleys, he finally felt that he had lost them………. at least for now.

He stopped for a moment to catch his breath and after wiping the sweat of his brown, he took out a flask from inside his coat pocket and took a big gulp of its content to calm his nerves and as he was about to repeat the process movement from his right caught his eye and he quickly bolted and aimed his crossbow in that direction.

But after getting a good look at the 'enemy' he realized that what he saw was in fact a large window and it was his own reflection in it that had caught his eye a moment earlier.

He took several tentative steps towards it and as he looked at the glass he started to wonder.

"Who is that man with the long unkempt hair, with his unshaven face, and dirty skin?"

"Who are you? You who drinks hard spirits like its water, you with the weapon in your hand, with blood on your conscience? "

"Are you really me?" he asked himself as he moved the fingers of his right palm towards the glass, to touch it, to confirm if the image was real and not just something in his mind.

His hand was a hairs length away when a loud explosion jolted him out of his reverie and he quickly glued his back against the wall and raised his crossbow to once more look for the enemy.

"The Empire's on my tail, fire and brimstone everywhere and instead of running I take the time to touch a window………I really am not suited for this…." he bitterly lamented to himself, as he carefully peered out of the exit from the alley and after assuring himself that it was clear he continued towards a safer location, well as safe as it can be since a galactic superpower's army was here and searching for him.

Back on the rooftop a squad had been sent to take the now vacant roof, after a short but tense sweep, they quickly reported back to their command, a few minutes passed and they received the order to hold their position.

While others advanced they all sat down to take a breather and have a meal, not the most hygienic thing to do with corpses all around, you but that was war for you and if things got rough they did have some fresh supplies.

This particular group of soldiers where a unit composed of different species, from different planets and they all had different forms, but they were all humanoid in shape and where in their first form.

"Looks like one of them got away ma'am." the corporal said to his sergeant.

"Bully for him then! This isn't battle, it's a slaughter!" the sergeant said to her squad.

"Well, the enemy's just irregulars and we're professional soldiers." one of the privates said as he was using a piece of destroyed rooftop as an impromptu table to prepare the squad's lunch.

"It's slaughter all right, but for us not them." the sergeant said and upon seeing the confused looks on her troopers face she added the following:

"The enemy is using this whole neighborhood as a fortress, why haven't we been given any siege equipment, like chariots, or artillery to level this place?"

"Well HQ probably doesn't want to admit that the enemy has such a strong position within this city." the other private of the squad who was using a different fragment of the destroyed rooftop as an improvised chair replied.

"Then don't admit it and give us the kriffing heavy equipment!" the sergeant added and got a good natured chuckle from her squad.

"But ma'am that would make us hypocrites!" the trooper at the table said in mock outrage at the idea.

"Imperials being hypocrites, what a shocker!" the corporal added and another round of laughter came from the squad.

The sergeant joined them as well, her mouth moved to give way to some laughter, when a spear came out trough it. While she fell to the ground, she managed to catch a glimpse of the enemy that had slayed her and as life was leaving the sergeant's body she managed to witness the fate of her squad before her time was up.

The attacker moved fast, slashing away at the group of soldiers who did not have time to properly react to the situation.

It took only a few seconds and the squad was all dead.

Who where they, what was their life's story?

Would anyone remember them, cherish their memory? That was something that war didn't know, nor did it cared, thus there they rested as the battle continued all around the district, in the name of war, of this insatiable force that looked on with indifference to the lives that were given to it as tribute for each moment of its existence, and only continuing to rage on as more meat was put in the grinder.

Maramanakama Imperial field command center.

9:07 Local Planetary Time

Prince Gelios, the governor of this sector of the Occupied Territories looked over the map of the district he was attacking. His troops were highlighted in green on the map and a large portion of it was covered with shaded areas that represented zones outside their pulsar's line of sight.

"Who would have thought that the terrorists would be capable of making a shadow field around this area!" General Bartolommeo, a Carunian whose race was humanoid with a bulldog-like appearance and brownish yellow skin said to the prince.

"Well, they're main strength is stealth, so I guess it makes sense that they would focus on it." Gelios replied as he rubbed his chin in contemplation of his next move.

"My lord, we have just received the following: *'Count Luper has been hit by an ice arrow and has been taken to the field hospital!'*" one of the staff officers informed him.

"Serves him right! Him and his lead from the front attitude, a lord does not do the work of a common soldier, and this battle has been going on long enough! Order the troops to initiate an offensive into the area!"

"But my lord the enemy is heavily entrenched here; if we order a charge we will suffer heavy casualties! We should at least wait a little while until the heavy armor is ready!" Bartolommeo said to him.

"Well, isn't that what soldiers are supposed to do? So let them do their duty and die for their country." Gelios said with a disinterested wave of the hand.

"As for the armor, we cannot risk it being caught in an ambush; the heavies will follow the infantry, who will act as bait and spotters for it." The prince added.

Bartolommeo had no choice but to carry out the orders and so the general gave the command to attack.

After gazing at how his troops were preparing to charge the rebels, Gelios turned his gaze towards the ceiling and saw that a spider was hanging down from it.

"You know that today many will die so you've come to feast on them, didn't you my eight legged friend? Well if that's true, just wait a minute and you will not be disappointed!" he thought to himself as he raised a glass of wine in the gesture of a toast to the spider as a wicked smile formed on his face.

The Dukhym district.

10:56 Local Planetary time.

Ahmaianos reached the headquarters of his resistance cell, which was an old warehouse, there he saw that like him, his surviving comrades were all red in the face from exhaustion, this was evident even though the marans had red skin as their defining characteristic, from that you could tell just how much of a struggle it was to just reach their hideout in one piece.

"How are things on your ends?" he said to what was left of their forces, which was not much when compared to what they started out with.

"The north side is blocked." Tubarin said to him, he was a man with spiky red hair and a voice which would fit on some street punk.

"So is the south side." Karamus added.

"The east path is guarded, along with the west path." Duburius said to Ahmaianos.

Usanthus, Paiamara, Barathamas, Daiamar and Maiamar also gave they're reports, which they all mainly consisted of such elegant words like: 'we are taffed', 'we're kirffed' and of course 'crap' was a very popular choice for such an occasion.

"Do we have enough strength to break through and escape?" Ahmaianos asked them.

At this nobody said a word and Ahmaianos had his answer.

Just then the doors slammed opened and the red battle armor which had earlier killed a whole squad of Imperials entered the warehouse.

It raised its hand and slammed a heavy metal box right in front on them, the box opened to reveal energy crystals and some enchanted weapons.

"I managed to take this from a few scouting parties I killed." the voice of Kalynka was heard from inside the armor.

"Good job Kalynka!" Ahmaianos said with a soft smile on his face and this managed to lift some of the grim atmosphere that was present in the room.

Just then a small beep was heard from one of their crystals, it was a sensor alarm indicating that the enemy had entered the outer perimeter of their street.

They all activated an old farview crystal that they had and looked at the area where the alarms went off, and were shocked to see a force of about 500 infantry preparing to enter the district, behind them at least 80 cavalrymen and two dozen war chariots where being prepared.

"This is crazy! I thought that more than three fourths of their soldiers where on a holiday furlough! Just how much firepower does one local patrol have?" Tubarin said in a burst of anger at just how great the difference in strength there was between them and the Empire.

"What do we do now?" Kalynka asked nobody in particular and silence reigned as the answer to her question. They were desperate people, trapped in a hopeless situation. They needed a miracle to escape with their lives and unknown to her Ahmaianos thought the same thing.

"Guys, I will use this armor as bait and draw them to me and while I keep them busy you all can slip away." she said and this surprised them all, they didn't know how to respond to this, that is until Tubarin showed them the ropes.

"Like hell you are! I for one am not going to let you go alone! We all knew that this may be how we would end up and I say we give those cursed Imperials hell before we let the-"

*BOOM*BANG**BOOM*BANG**BOOM*BANG**BOOM*BANG*

He was unable to finish his sentence as the sound of a heavy bombardment of fire and earth projectiles was heard in the distance and fell near their position. Akanthos then pressed a few commands on the control runes and the image changed to another part of the city, one where artillery units where positioned.

There they saw a squad of TRH 'Earth Breakers', machines that had eight spider like legs and on each leg was a wide flat disk on its tips to help distribute the weight of the vehicles over as wide a surface as possible.

They're main bodies were also disked shaped and positioned with their flat side horizontally, there were two seats on the right and left backsides of the main body where the operator and the gunner sat. Between the two seats was a third one which was slightly more elevated and housed the spotter and behind him was an even slightly higher raised forth seat where the commander sat. The whole disk was engulfed in a cage that emitted an energy that could take the form of any element in order to create a protective shield against any enemy attack.

 In front of the seats there was a circle formed out of crystals and runes with small pillars coming out from the circle's diameter, which leaned inwards to form a conic shape nicknamed the 'cooker', whose tip ended with the starting point of a long and thick cylinder that extended for several meters from the front of the 'Earth Breaker' and was at a almost 60 degrees angle and aimed towards the rebel's estimated location.

When the commander gave the order to fire, a small vortex of energy formed in the 'cooker', which after shifting into an appropriate element or combination of a several, it was transmitted through the tip of the 'cooker' and into an ammunition shell.

The moment it was ready the Earth Breakers fired its load and the projectiles flew on a high arching trajectory towards their target.

The light from the explosion was what the Maran rebels saw first, a moment latter it was followed by an ear shattering noise that was accompanied by a small earthquake, the Earth Breakers certainly lived up to their names!

They stood there for a moment just gazing at the site of the impact before a second blast jolted them out of there stupor and with dread now firmly gripped in their hearts they all started taking weapons from the box Kalynka acquired and headed off to face the enemy, knowing that they were most likely marching to their resistance cell's final battle.

Ahmaianos turned to his comrades and with a voice that was filled with regret at how they're end was near said:

"At least we go out fighting."

They all made their way out of their makeshift lair and onto the streets, taking up ambush positions.

Everyone was gazing towards the direction where they expected the enemy to come from and they were all mentally preparing themselves for the end.

Some prayed, others thought of their life's greatest joys, others of their loved ones, a few just gritted their teeth in fear.

Kalynka, who was the youngest amongst them copped by thinking of the armor she was wearing, which was an stolen old Imperial model, namely the BGY- 11 standard ground forces armor. It was painted red instead of the standard dark green color intended for use in the open country, the front and back sides of it where made into an angle pattern of about 40 to 45 degrees which ran from the neck down to ankles and the arm pieces where a sort of triangular shape across the forearms that was also designed to deflect arrows, swords and blows from any attacker.

The helmet was an elongated double pyramid shape with a short top, with one angle in the front and one in the back and the remaining two situated approximately over each ear, the first two where the sharpest angles of the bunch, the helmet covered the neck all the way down to the base, connecting it with the chest armor.

The eye slots where situated at about the middle point of the structure where the two halves of the pyramids met, it was just below the angle and this helped shield the eyes from the sun when necessary.

The interior was also designed with a double wall skeletal frame which created a sort of interior second wall that was what actually covered the user's body, creating a small empty space between the wearers flesh and the true body of the armor. This not only increased the chances of survivability if the armor was pierced but also provided thermal insulation, keeping the wearer cool in the summer and warm in the winter, a fact which she was grateful for whenever she looked at her sweating teammates.

'Say what you want about the damn imps, but they know how to make good war gear!' Tubarin had once boosted after they had obtained the armor and the majority had all given reluctant nods of approval, that is except for Kalynka.

"Nothing good ever comes out of the Empire, they are pure evil!" was her reply.

After all, why would they be here in someone else's country, stealing other people's resources, forcing their will on another nation and beyond the Maramanakama system where dozens of other star systems all of which had been stolen by the Empire from their rightful government!

But she quickly banished her anger, for as they looked out towards the street in front of their hidden positions they could see a convoy approaching. It was composed out of an Defender Mark 11 war chariot, flanked by what looked like a platoon of soldiers numbering about 20 in strength, and although each soldier was wearing a newer and deadlier model armor than Kalynka's, the chariot was the real terror.

It's body was grand, at least five meters wide, fifteen meters long and three meters in height, it was a towering war machine, design for mid to mid long combat, it's front had a sharpened arrowhead shape and in the case of this particular model spikes where coming out off its lower side, to help remove any obstacle in its path, on the top of its body laid a dome encrusted with magic runes from where it could launch shells like the Earth Breakers.

On both its side where a pair halftracks that moved this great beast forward and across any obstacle.

It was a weapon designed for frontal assaults and breakthroughs, though it was vulnerable against cavalry, since it was slow to maneuver and its dome had a low firing rate when compared with a war horse's speed, that could charge it before it got too many shot's at the enemy.

That little fact was of no consequence for Ahmaianos and his rebels who had no cavalry.

They did however have a few select words about the chariot's (and the troopers accompanying the vehicle) parentage and preference for bed companions, but no cavalry.

Ahmaianos took in a deep breath and was about to give the order to attack, when suddenly a powerful barrage of spears was hurled from the second floor of a building that was on the right side of the street the convoy was on, it hit the Defender right on the one area where it's armor was weakest and namely it's top.

The spears where all fire spears that exploded on impact, turning the mighty behemoth into a blazing coffin for its crew, the ones that did not hit the Defender where hurled at the infantry, killing almost half of the platoon in a fiery inferno.

The survivors quickly rallied on the other side of the Chariot from where the attack came and quickly started a counter barrage of arrows and spears, but as soon as they did that from the left side of the street a burst of magic struck them.

Earth golems emerged from the ground; these unnatural killing machines quickly struck the troopers from behind. The soldiers being distracted with the floor from where the attack had come from, did not notice them and where quickly cut down from behind, after completing its mission the golems expired as their magic was depleted and they crumbed into rocks and dust.

10:56 Local Planetary Time.

The rebels all stared eyes wide and mouths open at the carnage that happened before their eyes, but the so called 'silence' which was a word used loosely in its proper meaning since this was a battlefield, was broken by Tubarin.

"Something's up there on the second floor!" he shouted as a shaped appeared from where the initial deadly salvo was launched.

A form emerged from the building, it appeared to be humanoid in appearance, but as the smoke from the barrage cleared the shape retreated back into the mist and disappeared.

7, 38

"**Fire two salvos of several high caliber energy arrows west of your location with the green building as your target, but make sure they are fire and water arrows and launch them in that order.**" a voice on their windwaker crystals was heard saying.

"What! Who the hell is this?"Tubarin angrily said into the crystal.

"**The one who you where staring at a few seconds ago scholar, now if you please fire a few salvos west of your location at the green building, lest you lose the opportunity that is before you!**" the voice on the other end replied.

What followed was a cacophony of enquiries from the rebels in regards to that statement, until a great shout from Ahmaianos silenced the chaos.

"QUIET! Now you said that we would lose the opportunity, opportunity for what?" he asked.

"**For victory of course, also you have four minutes left.**" the voice replied nonchalantly, which made everyone's eyes bug out in amazement.

"Victory!?!Victory against the Empire!"Kalynka said, the words surprising her.

"Why the hell should we listen to you!?"Tubarin asked suspiciously.

"**You should listen since I'm the one who singlehandedly slaughtered a force you couldn't even scratch, and If you continue on your current path you will meet your end in annihilation, but if you do as I say you will win, it's that simple, also you now have three minutes.**" the voice replied.

"Who is this guy? What kind of crazy-"

"Start firing!" Tubarin said, but was cut off by Ahmaianos.

"You can't be serious, Ahmaianos!" he said, stunned at their leaders sudden order.

"What choice do we have, you saw what he did, so just do as he says!" Ahmaianos shouted desperately as they all lined their bows and crossbows and fired the respective volleys.

"Now what? We just wasted what little ammunition we had and made a lot of noise for nothing! That was just-"

"The enemy is moving away from our location!" Tubarin shouted but was stopped by Usanthus, who was looking at the portable farview he was carrying, which depicted the battlefield map.

This course of action surprised everyone, since none expected this turn of events.

"But, but why?" Daiamar said, stunned at what had just happened.

"If you look closely at your position, you will notice that you have just fired over a river, and that the green building shielded any eastern view of your location, that combined with the destruction of the platoon, will make the enemy presume that after destroying it you've moved west because of the energy signature." the voice replied.

"And since there is no direct crossing here and the enemy must think we are on the other side and they'll move down town to where the bridge is!"Kalynka added, amazed at what just happened.

"We kept our position hidden by making as much noise as possible and led the enemy on a wild goose chase!" Ahmaianos, thought to himself surprised at how obvious the answer was.

"There is no time to waste, you in the red battle armor go to point seven up river and jump at exactly ten minutes from now and not a moment too soon, the rest of you will head to the coordinates I am currently transmitting to your farview, I'll contact you all with further instructions latter on." the voice replied, and ended the transmission.

"Cocky kriffer, isn't he?" Tubarin said in anger, at the strange voice.

"Do as he says." Ahmaianos told them, and from his tone you could tell that he was in no mood to argue, he was after all the leader of their group and for the most part he was a casual and easy going one, but he could be very serious and scary when he wanted to be, so they all complied and Kalynka went to her respective point.

"This is deep water and this armor is not calibrated to fight under it, I'll drown if I jump!"

"What are you doing? If you don't jump now, you're friends will all die!" The voice said all of a sudden and to that Kalynka snapped to attention, the combination of an authoritarian voice that resonated with power behind it and the prospect of losing what was left of her friends made Kalynka loose her hesitation and most of her grasp of basic common sense and so she prepared to jump.

"Oh, Great Catcher preserve me, let my aim be true, my catch be bountiful, its prize be great!" Kalynka mentally said the ancient prayer of her people and then jumped into the water and in another act which was against all common sense and logic; instead of drowning she stopped her submersion at knee depth.

"There is something beneath the surface!" she thought to herself, as she felt that the ground or rather the water below her started to rise and Kalynka realized that she was on a submarine. As the hatch opened and a crew member came out of it to see what was happening, he was immediately slayed by the armored resistance fighter, she then proceeded inside where she finished off the rest of the crew.

"What is this thing doing in the river?"

"The surrounding area does not have train tracks and the roads are too narrow to properly supply the Imperial assault, so they are relying on the river for logistics, your comrades will be joining you shortly, you can consider what's inside the submarine a bonus for our future contract, suit up and after that I will contact you with further orders." the voice said.

"Wait! At least tell me your name; it's kind of odd to just call you the voice." Kalynka almost shouted that request to him.

"I'm Nobody." he replied and ended the transmission just as the status quo would start to change for this corner of the universe.

Volun 4 system, the Planet Volun 4, headquarters of the 378th corps.

Metternich exited the train and before him lay a sight which would have unnerved others; there was a gathering of what could only be describe as monsters in front him.

There was a Caracian, a gray skinned giant spider who had eight long legs to support its body and two additional limbs that where about half as short as the rest, the pair ended with hands that contained long retractable claws.

Beside it was an Eschimariom, a black long haired centaur like creature that had an eye patch over his right eye and a bushy beard.

A Calabenecan, a giant insect like humanoid with locust features was next, followed by the Tetremadian who looked like normal human but had four arms and piercing green eyes. A Melionarion, a being that was made out of thousands of small yellow insect like creatures was what followed.

Next to the Melionarion was a Galapagian, who had a turtle's body, a mouth filled with razor sharp teeth, a bipedal frame and two upwards curbed long tusks coming out of its mouth.

Then came a Tumescan, a great raptor like beast who was holding what appeared to be a lollypop in its mouth.

Finally there was a Caninian, a great black furred wolf like humanoid that ended this lineup.

They were all dressed in a uniform similar to Metternich and Adrian, and each had various medals pinned to his and her's chest.

Behind Metternich Adrian emerged, a smile on his plucked hen features as he was happy to see his old classmates once more, from behind the aforementioned knight, the scent of a very expensive perfume that indicated that the sentient in question was always prepared to look his best, probably for company of the opposite sex came and penetrated their sense, signaled that Buts was right behind them, magic pouring out of his head as he levitated several pieces of luggage down the ramp and towards the assembled lineup.

Who and what where these beings before him you may ask?

"My Lord, may I formally introduce ourselves, I am Commodore Third Class Horatia TJ Jackson of the first division, these are viscount Antonius de Palamese commander of the second, Valyria Treakle third division, Duke Oscar von Raqianus fourth division, Tarkan el Balamarus fifth division, Prince Georgaian vi Alontaire sixth division, Prince Dalius Augustus seventh division and finally Colonel Werner von Braun, who commands the Black Berets assigned to our fleet." the giant spider being known as Horatia said.

Metternich smiled, and gestured to the eagle like being and the magic wielding serpent behind him and said:

"A pleasure to meet you all, you already know Adrian my Knight, the one behind him is Butz my personal aide."

Who where these creatures, you may ask? Why they where his new fleet of course!

Extract from the book "Confessions, an Admirals tale volume I"

I exited the ramp and upon gazing at the collection of monster and freaks which I would eventually call my loyal soldiers, confidants, and right and left hands, I immediately fought down the growing urge to vomit and bolt out of the place at full speed, all the while making my way down the ramp towards my new command.

But what should have stricken me as odd was that they were in their First Form.

You see even then Imperials, unlike Republicans or those Federals have the ability to change between their native form (called the first form) and a humanoid shape, or multiple native forms if they have mixed parentage.

It was one of the many things which helped unite the various nations of the Empire and keep it together.

Even before the Imperium when two sentient species from different planets met; hostility towards the other is the first thing that comes to both their minds. It's not their fault, since for some strange reason sentients have a sort of built in biological programming against those who are different than them.

Long ago the Great Founder of the Empire and her lieutenants found a way to get over that and gave the nations that would make up the Empire what is now called the 'Blessing'.

As you know, the blessing allows Imperials to morph from their native shape to a humanoid one and back, the only notable indication between them and humanity is the fact that the skin retains the same pigmentation as their original bodies, and certain aspects like various distinctive facial features or in more extreme cases and extra pair of arms, legs and various other appendages remain.

This had three delightful advantages: one was that it was rather hard for them to hate their fellow sentient since the barrier of racial differences (barring a few divergence in skin color) was gone, and there was no more hostility because of that, or rather it was reduced from a mainstream mindset to more of a annoying and trouble making indie scene, but for the most part the hatred and desire to blame others for their misfortune because they were different was diminished for the majority of people; well except if you're a Republican or Federal, they always find some reason to pin the blame on you and not themselves.

The second was that, well let's face it, sentients have always had a preference for new and exotic things, exotic food, exotic toys, exotic company, and when you can have a pretty girlfriend from another planted that is a whole new 'motivation' for friendly relations!

Thirdly, as I said earlier it changed the nature of Xenophobia and hatred for what was different. All of a sudden the various species which would make up the Empire realized they had something in common and it was a whole galaxy that barring the exception of a few immigrants who would join them, had nothing in common with the Empire, and so they did what any good rational and moral civilization would do and namely unite and prepare for war against the foreigners that were not 'blessed'.

And as I said before thanks to the 'Blessing' if you call it that, there were three shapes that an Imperial could take.

*The First Form was their native one, the Second Form was the humanoid one, the Third Form is...........
Well, more on that later on.*

What was odd was the fact that as an unofficial tradition in the military, when someone new arrived at a unit the members of the welcoming party where usually in their second form.

The idea in case of the enlisted men was that: 'you're an outsider and you got to earn your place' and in case of officers it was a sort of sign of respect only attributed to worthy leader. Now back then I had a reputation as a hero thanks to the media, but so many others like myself had similar reps in the army, navy, space fleet and air force/fighter corps, so I probably shouldn't have received at that point in my carrier such an honor, for that was shortly before the part of my carrier which would thrust me into the most dangerous moments of my life and earn me the respect of the army and fleet and draw a big bullseye on my back for enemy armies.

The fact that they were all in their first forms suggested that they were actually glad to see me!

That was crackers, since as I mentioned before I wasn't that big a hero back then. That combined with the fact that my arrival had the added effect of depriving one of them of the opportunity for advancement in rank, meant that the current situation was so desperate that these poor buggers where either under the delusion that I could actually bail them out or they were glad someone was here to take the fall when the dam breaks!

I approached Horatia, and as she extended her right arm, I took what was an arachnid version of a hand complete with retractable claws in her chitinous fingers and shook it. I searched her eyes, all six of them for any sign of deception, hoping and praying 'Please God, let these people be lying to me, don't let them be actually glad to see me, let their happiness for my arrival be false, let the truth be that they hate me for coming here and stealing their chance for a promotion! Let them be bootlickers and ass kissers!', but much to my horror her smile was genuine in all of its fangy and venomous glory, and upon seeing the others up close and shaking hands with them as well I noticed that their smiles where more brighter, sincerer and happier than what I originally thought.

Dear God, the situation was a disaster! Heaven save me from their happy smiles!

Metternich per Pelasgiamus, Freelance Potions maker

After exchanging pleasantries, he was lead to a conference room where once everyone was properly seated, Metternich found himself next to Tarkan el Balamarus and Valyria Treakle with Butz behind him and Adrian next to Valyria.

On the other side of the table was Prince Dalius Augustus, Prince Georgaian vi Alontaire, Duke Oscar von Raqianus, Viscount Antonius de Palamese, and Baroness Horatia T.J. Jackson, next to them there was Colonel Werner von Braun, the leader of the ground forces, the famous 88th brigade of the elite Black Berets Corps, also called the 'Hellfire Knights'.

The 88th is considered by many to be one of the finest brigades amongst the Black Berets, some even said that it was one of the finest infantry units in the whole galaxy; one so strong than even the other Black Berets had trouble reeling them in.

Besides him sat the leaders of the space fighter squadrons, who were also the aces of the flying corps, namely Captains: Nagira Tadamaki, Ivan Molotov, Ataru Starstruck, Furio Figaretti and alongside them the many ship captains and squadron leaders.

"Our forces are placed in the following order from north to south: Dalius, Georgaian, Oscar, Antonius, Horatia, Valyria, my division and finally Von Braun's 88th make out the forces in this sector. Our opponents the Volunian Eight Army and the Federal Task Force have roughly the same numbers of troops and have fortified the Granada Depression, its southern flank is blocked by a mountain range and the northern one is blocked by the sea, so our only route of attack is a direct assault on their positions." Tarkan briefed Metternich.

"Also, there are only two energy nexuses on this planet, they control both of them, this enables the enemy to recharge their energy crystals, while we have to rely on warp trains to transport them here, giving them an advantage in a battle of attrition." Valyria added.

"What about siege units like dragon towers, they are specially designed for something like this, could we not used them against those defenses?" Adrian asked them.

"We do not have any towers, hell we don't even have enough mines to make a decent minefield for one of our divisions, let alone our whole front." Raqianus replied.

"One more question, how in the blue bloody blazes did this force here arrive to such a deplorable state!" Metternich asked in earnest, for you see from what he gathered from the briefing slate the Planet which they now resided was the only one in this system that could sustain life, and it along with Volun 1,2 and 3 where only an outposts for the World Class Fortress Galiana.

And so the original mission of the 378th corps had been to come here, blast the small garrison into oblivion, set up a planetary base and space port, wait until the enemies counterattack came, then withdraw back to their lines and draw the enemy for the main fleet to cut down.

You might think that such a mission would seem odd or even insane, to blow up some garrison and then just sit on down and do nothing but wait for the enemy to come and then run away.

 But this was a 'Moral Booster', a battle indented to be of small scale, but also designed to be a victory in order to raise morale amongst the troops and civilians, to mentally prepare them for the upcoming bigger battles and to also act as bait to draw an enemy from their entrenched position with a raid.

Metternich saw it for what is was and in his mind it had been the ideal command for him, here he would be the highest ranking officer, the destruction of the base would be enough to say he had done his duty and he could be relatively safe here, at least for the time being.

The only problem was that the planet had not been bombarded from orbit, the ships where now grounded all along their lines and used as anti-infantry weapons instead of being in space, and the enemy instead of being small dust particles where now heavily entrenched on the high ground in front of them.

He looked at his new command, since everyone was refusing to answer his enquire and stated his question once more.

"I repeat, how did we arrive at this sad state of affairs?"

After a few moments of hesitation, and a few quick words of help and praise to her deity Horatia spoke up.

"Upon arriving, we scanned the planet and discovered that the enemy garrison was actually at only 20 percent strength, and that those 20% percent where troops composed of reservists, many of them quite old by military standards." she then paused and even though it was difficult to see an expression on her arachnid features you could tell that she was now regretting being the one to begin the story.

"Continue Commodore." Metternich said in an encouraging and appreciative tone and looked to her expectantly.

"We were about to commence bombardment, when our commander Rear Admiral Cassius, stated that instead of destroying it we should capture the supply depo with an infantry assault." the voice of Antonius was heard saying and all of the gazes at the Eschimariom as he continued the story.

"But after we launched the assault, our troops were repulsed by the defenders."

"Wait a minute! Are you trying to tell me that Black Berets where repulsed by a group of senile bingo players!" Adrian's voice his opinion on the absurdity of the notion.

"Considering that those senile bingo players had a battalion of retired but recently brought back to active duty Holy Knights, I'd say that's exactly what happened." Werner answered his question.

This made Adrian's mouth fall agape, the Holy Knights where elite shock troopers of the Federation and since the Federation and the Volunians where close allies, this meant that their presence indicated that the Federation had now unofficially joined the fight between the Empire and the Volunians instead of just offering 'token' support.

Adrian looked at Werner still in disbelief and hoping that it was some lie, but Werner sadly only confirmed with his gaze that it was the truth.

"And after that what happened?" Metternich asked breaking the silence in the room and the semi starring contest between Adrian and von Braun.

"We then did the only sensible military action during this whole fiasco and withdrew the troops." Oscar replied. He then crossed his two pairs of arms and with a cold stare he used his gaze and body language to chide and visually reprimand those present for this inefficient report, but the only effect was more silence.

"What happened after that? And could one of you tell the whole story, since a standard day only has so few hours in it!" Metternich said, starting to lose his patients.

"The Admiral then ordered us to battle stations and used the ships to ram the enemy defenses." Dalius answered Metternich, with a cheery tone like it was a matter of fact.

"He.........he rammed the planet!?!You're kidding, aren't you?" the commander said in disbelief to what he just heard.

"Sorry Commander, I only tell a joke when it's funny, but I can tell a few now if you like." Dalius replied, his voice devoid of cheeriness.

"And everybody knows that this is the best moment to tell a joke!" Valyria said the tone of her voice indicated that the meaning of the phrase was very much a different one from its literal one; in short she was being sarcastic.

"Yes, we rammed the defenses, but the enemy being the enemy had the impudence to actually use their brains and withdraw to another position as they saw us coming; eventually after we hit dirt side, our power crystals where too drained from shielding the ships from impact to be any further use, so we deployed our ground forces in a defensive line facing the enemy." Tarkan said before Valyria and Dalius started arguing and looked at them sternly. He discreetly separated a few dozen of the small beings which formed his body and they started flying around him as he looked at them menacingly with all the hard gaze of a drill sergeant preparing to discipline two raw recruits which was not surprising since he was a master sergeant before becoming an officer, it got the point across and they settled down and gazed away from each other and from Tarkan in particular.

After that, all eyes were on Metternich who was rubbing his temples as a headache started to form.

"The situation is bad sir, but it could have been worse, the ships despite being drained are still battle worthy, morale is surprisingly high since every soldier and sailor heard you where coming and we have enough ammunition and fuel four one good infantry scrap." The tusked mouth of Georgaian said as the somehow heavy atmosphere in the room slightly improved

Finally after what seemed like an hour, although scarcely a few seconds had past, Metternich found his voice.

"And where is the former commander now?" Metternich asked.

"He hosted a feast weeks ago, to celebrate our 'upcoming victory' over the enemy fleet, so he drank, and drank, and drank, till he drank his final cup and since the other leaders all have the ranks of commodore with equal seniority, we did not have someone else to take over command, and where uncertain what to do, that is until you came sir." Antonius replied and gave an honest smile, which unnerved their new commander, since it help punctuate just how deeply their where krifed and where desperately looking for a way out or a fall guy.

"Why haven't they attacked us with their ships?" Metternich asked.

"Their gearing up for that, our most recent Intel says the fleet of Admiral Yemen is on his way here." Georgaian answered him.

"Also, the enemy has been receiving a constant stream of reinforcements since we've tried to ram them, currently they outnumber us." Antonius told with reluctance.

"But not by a large margin, for now they just have about an estimate 10-15% advantage in terms of numbers, still within a manageable range for us." Georgaian added to the conversation.

"Nuts, to our side then!" Metternich said cheerfully, with what seemed to be a hollow and humorless laugh as he looked over the map.

"No chances for a promotion here sir." Werner said with a smile on his face, intentionally provoking the newly minted commander.

The other high ranking officers chided him for his words, with the exception of his subordinates within the 88th, namely Major Casper Lintz, whose species the Goy where white skinned and pale with notably longer than usual fangs but with a humanoid body, Captain Montpellier who was a Colian, a humanoid amphibious species, a fact made more evident by his scales, long dolphin like snout, fins on his head, membrane fingers and most notably a sort of reverse diving helmet which had its own reserve of water.

And Lieutenant Jericho McClelland, whose species the Catcherfizer was very much human looking, with the exception of the fact that his race had the ability to reattach severed limbs and survive great wounds that did not include injuring one particular organ and namely the brain. As a consequence of that the surface of his skin was riddled with scars, so very much so that it was hard to tell where the scars ended and where the normal skin began.

They were used to their commanders behavior and where unfazed by it.

But for Adrian, that was an almost inexcusable insult to his liege and he looked ready to jump out of his seat and strike Werner, the Black Beret only match his stare with a smile on his face that said a non verbal challenge of 'come and get it!'.

"Oh, what a disappointment!" Metternich said with faux shock and a great deal of mostly comical exaggeration to those present and they replied with laughter, which helped defuse the tension in the room and stop the staring contest between Adrian and Werner.

"Colonel, you have never seen my shock and disappointed face, have you?" he added with a stony, emotionless expression on his face, and after von Braun shook his head the newly minted commander deadpanned with:

"Now you know it." using the same statue worthy expression and in a dry tone which drew more laughter from those present, even Werner gave a healthy chuckle.

After it died down Metternich took another look at the tactical display.

His gaze studied the map and it was a most distressing sight since the enemy had both flanks secure, strong fortifications and with Yemen coming they were running out of time, but as he studied the display he saw something which could give them the much needed situation reversal.

"And a potential glorious destruction, of myself and this whole fleet!"

He thought to himself, as his guts started to hurt, which was the reaction his body made when something like this happened. He could have ignored it and simply ordered a general withdrawal trough the warp portal and scuttle the warships, but if he did that it would haunt him for the remainder of his life, which could be a very short time, especially since he knew from his years in the fleet that there were some commanders who would bravely defy all logic and reasoning and no matter how sound and wise a withdrawal like that would be, they would still send him back to retake the ships and without reinforcements to boot. So despite his natural tendency to avoid battle he kept his gaze on the area of the planet where he knew the decisive one would be fought. For just south beyond the mountains on the enemies left flanks was a forest, one of the densest forests on the planet.

"We could bypass the mountains and go through the forest and attack from the rear." Metternich.

"Sir, I would endorse such a plan but the forest in too thick, how could we move the troops trough it?" Horatia asked.

"Here is how." he replied and he told them his method.

"We still have enough resources for that, but may I remind you that if we are discovered, not only are we in danger of having the flanking force ambushed, but since the initial phase would use up most of heavy equipment, the distraction force would be vulnerable to a counterattack." Werner said to those present quick to point out the great danger of this plan.

"Also even if we manage to do it, if we do not capture the supply dump, almost half of our troops will be isolated in enemy territory without supplies and destroyed, we cannot afford the loss!" Valyria added.

"And with our lines so thin, our forces that remain here could be cut to pieces if the enemy counterattacks, which I am certain any decent commander would do, even with the danger of him hitting the ships and starting a chain reaction." Tarkan added.

At this Metternich closed his eyes for a minute, hoping that somehow he could block what he knew he was about to say.

"What you have all said is true and doing this plan would put us in immediate jeopardy, but in our current situation the enemy has a logistical advantage over us and with a fleet inbound we have little choice in the matter, it's conquer or die." He paused, stood up from his seat and with his arms crossed behind his back walked several feet away from the table, and after a moment of silence he added the following:

"If we execute this plan, there is a great risk of defeat and destruction within a week, but if we do not, then certain destruction await us within the coming month, or capture and then God knows what's next! I don't know about you fellow sentients, but when compared to being taken by the Federation, the idea of death in battle doesn't sound so bad." he added for once he was speaking the truth, or perhaps the truth a soldier of his reputation was expected to say.

At this not a word was spoken within the room, the grim reality of the situation Rear Admiral Cassius had landed them in left them speechless, the silence lended itself to an unspoken agreement to execute the plan, even Werner who was known to be skeptical and indifferent to fleet commanders (that almost got him court marshaled a few times), had nothing to say for it was hard to find faults in the cold heard truth of reality.

So he had a different kind of contribution to the conversation.

"Commodore, I have a purely speculative question which I'd like you're opinion on." Werner asked and Adrian tensed at that, as if knowing that the colonel would continue with his provocation of Metternich.

"If, from a purely theoretical point of view, I would call you a glory seeking jackass, who only got his rapid promotion because the Warchief sponsored you and that you're name of Hero of Marengo was a just a fluke, what would be your response?" Von Braun asked.

"COLONEL DO YOU WISH TO BE FLOGGED!!!!" Adrian angrily shouted from the top of his lungs, his arm going to the hilt of his sword, he looked poised to attack Werner over the Colonel's gross breach of protocol and great disrespect to a superior officer, von Braun remained unfazed and simply smirked.

Metternich, despite having a look of anger of almost the same caliber as his knight did on his face, raised his hand to stop his subordinate from escalating the conflict, which seemed to partially calm Adrian down, as he let go of his sword hilt but not before adding:

"I was at Marengo sir, and I assure you that was no fluke!" the hatred for Werner was evident in his eyes as he sat back down.

But this was quickly forgotten by those around the table, as they all gazed at Metternich to gauge his reaction and a collective holding of breath was taken when he finally spoke.

"To your question Colonel, my response to your 'speculations' would be that 'from a purely speculative point of view' you will be denied lunch rations and that you will receive none at dinner." Metternich said, and everyone where uncertain how to react at this, they expected Werner to be flogged or worse, not simply be sent to bed without supper for being a naughty boy.

Von Braun who was equally surprised as the others looked ready to point out the fact, but before he could say anything Metternich continued with:

"And if the colonel adds any more, he will be denied four days worth of rations."

"You would deny the commander of your most elite infantry unit food right before a major operation?" Werner said, astounded at just how merciful one moment the punishment seemed to be and just how cruel it was the next.

"No Colonel, you will be the one to deny the aforementioned officer four days worth of food, so what happens next is entirely you're responsibility." the Commodore said and gazed with his red eyes at Werner, the color and intensity growing with each passing moment of silence, making even the hardened infantry commander starting to feel 'uncomfortable' under that burning stare.

"Understood sir! And thank you for answering my 'speculations'!" Werner said with a cheerful and friendly smile on his face, not the reaction one would expect when threatened with starvation.

"I want all preparation to be finished as soon as possible, how soon can we commence the operation?" Metternich asked after a few moments of silence.

"I'd say about 72 hours my lord." Tarkan replied to him.

"Make it 48, also I'll be part of the flanking attack, since that will be the decisive fight will take place I will need to be present, I am not saying that Tarkan, Werner or Adrian cannot lead it, but I must be there for morale purposes."Metternich added which did make him grow in the eyes of his new subordinates since he willingly placed himself in the most dangerous area of the upcoming battle.

"And if things go rotten I can use that wood to properly exit stage left." he thought of the real reason he wanted to be there and kept it to himself.

"My lord shouldn't you address the troops?" Valyria asked the commander.

"Actions speak louder than words Valyria and in two days I intended to make this whole solar system tremble!" he said to her in a dramatic fashion, deciding to show the image of a brave, flamboyant and dashing commander, even though he didn't consider himself one.

"Also the idea of making one big battle speech, right before a supposed secret attack, sounds like, oh......
.........what's the proper word for that kind of idea?" he added with a soft smile on his lips, which indicated he was waiting for someone else to give the punch line.

"Nuts, commander?" Adrian added with a big smile on his face.

"Yes, that's the one! Whether it's the state of mind, or the fruit, it's the appropriate word."

Metternich said and a small collective chuckle was heard from the room, and as he got up to leave everyone else in the room gave a crisp salute, with the exception of Werner who gave halfhearted almost mocking salute which seemed to challenge Metternich to earn that from him, and instead of the desired effect of anger or of a indignation, the end result was only a few private homicidal thoughts from Metternich towards the Colonel, before turning around and leaving.

The junior commanders also left the room, all with the exception of Tarkan and Valyria.

"So that's the man of the hour, Metternich per Pelasgiamus, what is your opinion of him Valyria?" he asked her.

"He knows how to lift a person's spirits and he seems to have some degree of intelligence and wisdom in him, also he's right, if we do not do this risky plan, we may not live to see home once more." Valyria added with a small touch of nonchalance.

"And if his plan fails?" Tarkan asked, his voice filled with curiosity.

"Then this entire fleet corps and Black Beret brigade either dies in battle, from hunger, thirst or is captured and taken to a prison camp." Valyria gave a deadpan reply.

"That's not a very pleasant thought; shouldn't you have a more optimistic look on the future? You could learn a thing or two from Georgaian!" Tarkan asked with a chuckle.

"My look on life is a realistic one, it's not my fault that our reality is such garbage and I wouldn't want to step on Georgaian's toes, especially since his toes have razor sharp talons on them." she said with a smile on her lips.

Tarkan gave a nod of acknowledgment, after which he got up from his seat and left to start working on the plan.

As he walked, thoughts of the battle ahead where weighing heavily on his mind, for he had never anticipated than when they had left their base for Volun 4 on nothing more than a small 'Moral Booster' that it would devolve into such a desperate struggle and risky operation and the thought of dying in the land of the Empire's enemies filled him with worry.

"What the hell, no guts, no glory!" he said out loud to himself, in order to alleviate his troubled mind, as he took a small mirror from his pocket, looked over his uniform and made a mental notes to change it before the battle with a new one, if he was going to die in the next battle, he would go out in style!

Sergeants must look their best all of the time, especially sergeants turned officers!

In another section of the command center Colonel Werner and his subordinates were sitting down at table having a meal.

"That was a bit out of line Colonel, even for us." Lintz said to him.

"Maybe ,but it was necessary for me to get a good idea of our new commander, after all we only know the guy for a few hours and we're supposed to let him gamble with our lives!" Werner added as he took a sip of coffee.

"And what did you gauge from his reactions?" Montpellier asked.

"He got angry at my remark and refused to take the bait, that means he can control his emotions and impulses, he uses a punishment that fits the crime, he also made it so that I would get at least part of the blame from the troops, so that means he knows how to win a situation and avoid at least a part of the fallout from it, a good start but for now he is still on probation." von Braun replied.

"Do you think we will be alright with him, he's rather young for a commodore, I mean he's barely in his late to mid twenties." McClelland asked.

"Good question, I do not want another Cassius on our hands!" Lintz added and nearly spat on the ground in disgust, and considering his mouth was full with mustered fried pork and mashed potatoes, that was probably a good thing.

"If he turns out to be another Cassius, then we can always organize another banquet." Werner replied coldly, as they all continued to dig in to their lunches.

Werner got a forkful of meat and potatoes, but just as he was about to take a bite he stopped, placed the fork back on his plate and pushed the plate away.

 He then laid back in his chair and simply continued to sip the coffee, the others noticed this and we're surprised by it, but decided to say nothing about it, they only continued with their meal.

Maramanakama Imperial field command center.

12:23 Local Planetary time

"*Damn this summer heat, its hot enough to fry meat on the side walk, this whole city could use a river, no, a lake running through its streets!*" Gelios who was comfortably sitting in his chair thought to himself as he wiped the sweat from his forehead, watching as the first wave of his attack entered the enemy's territory; he was confident in the notion that success was guaranteed, when suddenly one of his staff members said the following:

"Sir, third squadron was ambushed and destroyed!"

"What?" Gelios said as he quickly got up from his chair and walked to the battle map, as he looked at it he saw the small images of his units disappear one by one.

"Eight squad is under assault."

"Second squad is retreating."

"Forth squad has just been ambushed from behind and we've just lost contact." The orderlies said to their lord.

"We are getting reports of raids on the field hospital's defenses!"

"What the hell is going on out there?" Gelios shouted in a mixture of anger and surprise.

378th command headquarters, Metternich's private room.

*"Kriffing bum, judging me like that without even knowing me!"*The young commodore thought to himself as angrily slammed his fists on his desk, several hours had passed since the meeting and he was going over the files of the 88th and the intelligence reports from CORSEC, at least that was what he was doing up until now, when for some unknown reason the meeting flashed through his mind, making him angry at a lot of things, at the war, at Werner, but especially at himself for not being able to avoid all this madness.

He continued to frown at nothing and nobody for a few minutes, until his anger disappeared and silent tears threatened to trickle down his face.

"I might have made an enemy of the most dangerous Imperial on the planet, tomorrow I will prepare for not just a battle but a decisive one, the day after I might die! I should run, run away from this war, from this madness, from people killing others by thousands each day." He thought to himself as he lay on his bed and activated the rune spells on his ceiling, which made the night sky appear on it.

"Maybe if I did others would follow, the officers, the enlisted men, maybe just maybe the enemy would do the same, we could all go far away, like the Great Founder Tomiris did, let the Field Marshalls and Admirals and politicians have their war, let them fight and starve and die!" Metternich thought to himself and a flicker of hope spread across his face, before cruel reality removed it from him.

"No, that will not happen, I could hardly desert when I was starting as a captain, and now with my face well known and my reputation, it's impossible for me to go undetected, I have thousands of men from my new command watching me , also even if I tried to desert they would never follow, for I know we fight wars because of pride, greed, shame, and the greatest reason off all stupidity, and from my time as a potions maker I know that those are the few ailments that we do not have a cure for." he thought to himself as he exhaled a disappointed breath of air as he got up from his bed and went to make a few rounds across his new command.

He had a meal in the enlisted personal's mess hall, he chatted with soldiers and sailors all who were very happy to have the 'Fox of Marengo' as their new commander, after that was finished he went back to his quarters to try and get some sleep.

He barely got any sleep at all, so he just got up and went for a second round, and a third and fourth and twelfth, his stomach was aching from nervousness for the battle ahead, preventing him from resting.

He knew that he had already checked everything and gave the necessary orders at the meeting, but he was a very agitated person and because of his stomach and from past experiences he knew that for the next few hours he would not be able to sleep.

So he continued his rounds, not just to help calm his nerves and diminish his anxiety, but also because stuff like having the commander be seen and interacting with the troops would improve moral, and it helped if the enlisted men appreciate their commander, since you would want several thousand men and women with deadly weapons to like you, wouldn't you?

The Dukhym district

12:48 Local Planetary time.

"Numbers 3 to 6 attack now!" The voice of Nobody ordered over the windwaker airways.

On his command the fourth imperial squadron was destroyed.

"Excellent, now numbers 2 and 8, set several fire arrows at location 43-87, numbers 9 and 3 will fire at the same location with winter ice water arrows, numbers 5 and 10 proceed to point four and fire at the eight o clock direction, also number 4."

"Y-yes!" Kalynka asked, since she was the designated number 4.

"Since you are apparently the ace pilot here, this is what I want you to do, move to location 78-49, at my command I want you to temporarily deactivate the cloak field spell." Nobody replied.

"But that will make them send all of their forces at us!"

"One needs proper bait for a great trap, you've trusted me so far, do as I say and our victory will be complete, as for the rest of you I'd like you all to do the following……" he replied with and transmitted his orders.

Those present hesitated for a moment, but only for a moment and they then carried out his commands, The battle was starting to go in their favor and they where to drunk on winning to object, at least for now.

Maramanakama Imperial field command center.

12:53

"Sir, the eastern bridge has just collapsed taking the second company with them!"

"Our submarine pool has just been heavily damaged; looks like one of our own subs just did a suicide run!"

"The reinforcements from the northern side have been ambushed and pushed back outside, also we are getting reports that the enemy is using battle armors!" the orderlies said to Gelios.

"It must be the Maran Liberation Army or the Marans People's Front; they're the only ones amongst the terrorists that have battle armors!" Bartolommeo said to his liege.

"It can't be him……..It can't be Alefran, can it?" Gelios asked with concern in his voice, Alefran was one of the most feared of the rebel leaders in the Maran sector.

"Sir, the enemies cloak has just fallen!" one of the tactical officers said to his commander and the prince looked at the display and saw as the enemy units position was revealed.

"Ha! There they are! They're in the center of the district, now we have them! All units charge!" Gelios ordered.

"But my lord, doesn't it seem suspicious that-"

"Shut your mouth Bartolommeo, they have made a fool of me long enough, I want every warrior on them now!" Gelios cut him off with a shout, and his order was carried out.

The Dukhym district

"The enemy is now advancing on your positions, all units I want you to maintain your current status and do not engage the enemy as they pass you, I repeat your main objective is to remain hidden, also number 7, are you ready?" Nobody asked.

"My name's Tubarin, and yeah I'm in position." Tubarin replied.

The Imperial chariots and support units made their way through the streets, unknowingly passing the rebels, who where now hiding, after they reached the center of the district where their map told them the enemy was an order was given to Ahmaianos's group.

"Now number 7 initiate the spell!" Nobody ordered him.

Maramanakama Imperial field command center.

13:01

"Sir, the troops have reached the center and are reporting that the only thing there are some power crystals that are blasting away their energy." one of the orderlies reported.

*BANG*BOOM***BANG*BOOM***BANG*BOOM***BANG*BOOM**

"What the hell was that?" Gelios asked as explosions were heard coming from Dukhym.

"Incoming emergency transmission, I'm putting it trough."

"This is lieutenant Brandon of the 27th squadron, HQ the sewer below us has just collapsed some of us have been taken down by it, the rest are fighting the torrent of water within it, request……………." his report was cut off by the sound of him screaming and then only static remained to be heard from the communication crystal.

"It's Alefran, Alefran is here!" Gelios said as fear started griping him.

"Sir, the enemies cloak has been reactivated!"

The Dukhym district.

13:03

"Looks like……….the enemy is retreating!" Kalynka said with a smile and look of astonishment on her face at how easily the mighty Empire was repulsed and how simple yet completely under their noses the tactics they used where.

Making noise to cloak your position, using your forces in irregular firing patterns, maintaining a flexible front, using bate and trap tactics, these where all easy and effective tactics.

They were just not something that most people could come up with from the top of their heads.

That and having the enemy's stolen armors and Nobody on your side was a plus in her opinion.

"All units break through the encirclement, with their forces in temporary disarray they shouldn't be much of a threat to you, but that won't last for long, after you get to safety I suggest you lay low for a while, you may keep the armors as a gift, one of many more are to come."

"You have all lived up to my expectations, I will contact you latter to finish the contract and negotiate the payment for future services." The voice of Nobody told them.

"Wait, just who are you?" Kalynka asked through the communication crystal, but only static came from it.

Volun 4, the position of the 378ᵗʰ.

Month of Caliupus, 10ᵗʰ

5:52

"Is everything in position Adrian?"

"Ye my lord, we just await you're order." He replied

"Very well, the sun's about to come up so you may give the signal for the attack, no sense in wasting the cloak of darkness since we'll need all the help we can get." he ordered and Adrian nodded and left to occupy his respective post in the upcoming battle.

Metternich plan was simple, Valyria along with Horatia, Oscar, Dalius, Antonius and Georgaian would begin a frontal assault on the enemy, while at the same time the forces of Tarkan and Werner which were now lead by their new commander would perform a pincer maneuver from behind after crossing the forest south of the mountains.

He walked towards where Butz was waiting with their spider-wolf jeep, and after getting into the gunner's seat he took a picture from his pocket.

It was taken only a month before the pirate incident that got him shanghaied into the navy, in the picture where his friends who were also his original crew, they were from all over the galaxy but all were happy and smiling.

Nostalgia gripped him as he gazed at his old life, before that fateful day when it was changed forever, before the war, before they all left to fight each other.

He gazed at his old friends, his eyes lingering on Jonathan who had left them that day to pursue other ventures.

He missed the old days, Jonathan in particular for he was his best friend.

"This is it Jonathan, another day, another battle, I'll win it or at least make a big enough mess to run away from it, wish me luck and I hope you are all alright." he said to himself and he placed the picture back in his pocket as all around him his command started the assault, and with that the battle armor he was wearing all of a sudden became very, very heavy and uncomfortable, and his stomach started aching again as anxiety for the battle gripped him .

The uniform he had been wearing was still beneath that armor. He was wearing the newest model battle armor, namely the AP2- 587 and like its predecessor the BGY, it was about the same shape, but with a few improvements such as various hooks and rings across its body to make it very customizable in terms of what the wearer could carry, it had an internal heater and air conditioner which helped maintain the comfort of the wearer.

Its surface skin had a special rune spell imbedded into it that allowed it to change colors, making it an essential feature for ambushes and remaining undetected by the enemy.

The armor carried an oxygen extractor for underwater breathing, and an air pack for zero G space combat if necessary.

Metternich's armor was the same model the rest of the Imperial army used, with the exception that his shoulders where lined with fur and he strangely wore a leather long coat over his armor, one that reached down to his feet.

Metternich's helmet was also unique, in that it was a cylindrical shaped one that encased his head, the helmed was a dark golden-coppered color and had a series of circle like bumps that covered most of its surface, the shapes where clearly designed to divert and deflect sword blows from the wearer's head.

At forehead level, a sculpture of a pair of eyes was encrusted into the design; its purpose was according to the ancient beliefs of his ancestors to ward off evil and danger.

Also the back of the helmet that was at eye level together with the sides that protected the ears had sculptures of battles his people had fought with their four holy weapons: the bow, the saber, the falx-falcata and the two retiarius weapons, and though he did not consider himself a warrior he could do a decent job with his ancestor's sacred tools.

The helmet was made to be serviceable, intimidating, to shown one's rank to the ally without alerting the enemy and above all to ensure its users survival.

That and it looked pretty sweet!

But he had no time to ponder his battlefield fashion choice, since the battle itself was about to begin, so he clasped his hands, closed his eyes and prayed.

"God in heaven, help me and my army and navy, please give me strength to survive and see to it that as many of my warriors as is possible survive this battle, also.................also please make sure that as few foes die as well, and for those that do, be they enemy or Imperials, please make sure they do not suffer and forgive them and us for what we are about to do." he prayed to his God, made the holy signs of faith and piety and then turned his now opened his eyes to what lay before him.

Above him the roar of the clouds was heard, as a storm was brewing and despite himself Metternich gave out a smile of relief, for the storm could help mask their attack!

He opened his eyes as the thunder from heaven was joined by the thunderous roar of hundreds of earth breakers and chariots that opened the battle.

The fight for Volun 4 had begun!

Volunian/Federation Southern flank.

5:52 Local Planetary time.

The members of the 1st squadron of the 695th fighter regiment were exhausted and weary, not just of the fact that most of them where from sub temperate climates and they were in a desert like area, but also of for the fact that their current commander Lt Lance Hendrickson was dragging them along Captain Hannibal Rogue's extended patrol mission.

"Why in the name of all that is holy are we here?" Bob one of the foot soldiers asked the others around him.

"Our regiment is here because the Volunians are allies of the United Federation of Planets (U.F.O.P), and we are here to protect them from the Empire." Hogan replied.

"I'm not talking about that, I'm talking about why are we going each night on an extended patrol here of all places? I mean we're dozens of miles away from our front lines, that and we're fliers not ground pounders, also there's nothing here but the entrance to that forest!" Bob said to him.

"Well, that's what we get for having Hannibal 'Silly Billy' in our regiment; the crazy fool actually thinks the enemy will come from behind us! What's next? Will their monarch do a triple summer salt, land on our right and left flank and moon us to death?" Hogan said and the others around him chuckled, they had little respect for their current highest ranking officer, since his latest proposals had been time and time again rejected by their senior officers for being too outlandish. The generals had even gone as far as to reprimanding him publically and they had even begun a not so secretive smear campaign, making him the laughing stock of both armies stationed on Volun, they they he had done decent job at that since it made the troops forget the fact that he was once the most popular and well respect sailor in the fleet that was stationed here.

"They're laughing at you, should I do something about it?" Lieutenant Hendrickson asked Hannibal, Lance had a good ear and could clearly pick up what the soldiers were saying behind their backs.

"Let them be kid, I'd rather them be right and laugh at me than it be the other way around; I just hope I'm wrong." Hannibal replied to the young freckle faced Lance as they started climbing the small hill that was before them.

Hannibal was about eight years older than the twenty something Lance, but despite their age difference the two men got along well, almost like brothers.

As they were nearing the top of the hill Hannibal asked Lance the following:

"So how are things at home?"

"Same old, same old, Miranda's got another suitor pursuing her."

"And how many beaus does that make, fifteen?"

"Thirteen actually." Lance said and both men shared a chuckle, Miranda was Lance's twin sister and the object of affection from many of the young men back at the capitol.

Miranda and Hannibal had talked face to face over the windwaker and warprider a few times when Lance called home and they were at each other throats the moment they started chatting to each other.

They argued about anything and everything!

"You two are like oil and fire, put them together and it burns everything in sight." Lance teased him.

"We're not that bad!" Hannibal replied trying to sound insulted, but in fact he was trying hard not to laugh.

"Not that bad! At one point you argued about which brand of dung would be the most suited for growing jiga fruit."

"So?"

"Neither of you knew what jiga fruit even was at the time!" Lance countered with a smile on his face.

"We were merely making an intelligent debate based on speculations from general horticultural knowledge."

"Jiga is an underwater plant that grows in water so deep that sulfuric volcanoes are its only source of nutriments." Lance to his friend, a smug smile on his face.

Hannibal said nothing, merely shook his head in defeat.

"Why all of the sudden interest in my family?" Lance asked him.

"No reason, just making conversation and I have no interest in regards to your family whatsoever!" he replied.

"Or, maybe you have an interest in a particular member of my family." Lance said continuing to tease his friend as they arrived at the top.

As soon as Lance finished his sentence Hannibal quickly jumped on Lance and threw the young man to the ground, and so the lieutenant found himself with his back pressed against the dirt and with Hannibal on top of him.

"You know, when I said you had an interest in one member of my family this isn't what I had in mind!" Lance said to him in a confused and panicked voice but was cut off by Hannibal's hand which covered his mouth; he was about to struggle free when he saw that Hannibal was signaling with his free hand to be quiet and that there are enemies near.

Realization dawned on Lance and he gave a quick nod of his head, Hannibal released him and gestured to the crest of the hill.

Lance rolled on his stomach and followed Hannibal as they crawled to the top of the hill to look at the other side, the rest of the men that were with them followed suit.

When they arrived at the top and saw what was on the other side they could barely believe their eyes, all except Hannibal who cursed himself for being right.

Down in the valley where thousands of imperial soldiers and all of them were moving North West to attack their army's flank.

"This is impossible, that forest is too thick to move an army through!" Bob said to his teammates.

"Nothing is impossible kid, just hard to pull of sometimes; this here proves it and I got a sneaky suspicion that I know just how they did it." Hannibal said to him as he looked at the vast army before him.

"They're just a few miles away from our supply dumps; we have to do something before it's too late!" Lance said to Hannibal.

"It's already too late, look at that column over there." he replied, handing him a pair of binoculars.

"What do you see beyond it?"

"Supply trucks." Lance said to Hannibal.

"Exactly and supply trucks are usually placed where you least expect them to be attacked, which means that the enemy's rear is here and its spearhead is over there where our supplies are." he pointed towards the direction of their supply dumps.

As he was gesturing towards their own lines a sudden flash of light was seen in the distance, it was from a bolt of lightning which hit the ground only a few shorts miles from their locations.

As the sound of thunder echoed throughout the landscape the small group saw some movement below the crest and an enemy soldier walked towards them, they remained glued to the ground hoping the night would camouflage them so as to avoid detection, since there were countless enemies at the bottom of the hill and only a handful of them.

The soldier stopped just in front of Hannibal and stood there for a few moments, a sound was heard coming from the soldier and initially they thought that he was drawing his sword, but a moment latter Hannibal felt warm liquid pouring over his head and he realized that the soldier in question was relieving himself.

"I've heard of Imperials getting pissed at the Federation, but this is ridiculous!" Hannibal thought to himself as he fought down the urge to strike.

Lance upon seeing his friends 'predicament' moved his hand to his mouth to suppress his laughter.

After he finished urinating the soldier was preparing to return back to his post when another thunderbolt lit the night sky to reveal the U.F.O.P soldiers and a very angry and a very pissed captain, but before the soldiers had time to scream or call for help, Hannibal leaped up and stabbed the soldier in the gut, killing him and dragging his body over their portion of the crest as the sound of thunder roared across the land once more.

"That tonur! In combat you're supposed to use the sword given to you by the army, not the one given by Mother Nature!" Hannibal said is a half hushed voice as he dragged the body.

"Well, not everyone is as wise as you are!" Lance teased him.

"Kid save the jokes for latter, for now get the two wise guys behind us to send a warning to headquarters on what the enemy is doing, and let's get out of here." Hannibal said to them as the two in question jumped at the realization their commander knew that they had been badmouthing him behind his back.

But before they could say anything in their defense the communication crystal on the enemy soldier that had just been killed was heard broadcasting a message.

"Troop 17 report in, what's the situation?" The voice from the other end of the communication crystal said in Imperial Basic, and upon hearing they all froze in fear realizing that they may share the fate of this member of troop 17.

"Is everything alright?"

The occupied Territories, Maramanakama.

5:59 Local Planetary time

Kalynka and the others that had barely managed to escape the enemy's encirclement were now deep in another part of the city and away from harm. They were in one of their safe houses and were having a little celebration/wake for the battle and their fallen comrades, hugging and giving each other a pat on the back. Kalynka who was just as cheerful and at the same time as sad as the rest of them walked towards Ahmaianos who was in a corner away from the main festivities and as she approached him she noticed he was crying.

"Hey is everything alright?" she said with concern in her voice.

"Don't worry about me, I'm okay, I thought that today we would all die…..because of me……if we hadn't raided that column a week ago, this wouldn't have happened………..the others would still be alive." he replied half elated and half in sorrow.

"We all decided to do that raid and we all decided to stay and fight here, what happened today wasn't your fault!" she said and gave him a hug to reassure him that everything was alright.

"Looks like we had 'Nobody' to thank for that, whoever he is I thank the Great Catcher for him!" Ahmaianos said and returned the hug from Kalynka, he then got up and went to join the other in celebration, regardless of who this mysterious figure was, or how he managed all that had transpired today, one thing was certain namely that although the immediate future had up until this point always seemed to be bleak for them, now for the very first time there appeared to be a silver lining, a way of salvation for them and their people.

Volunian Federation Southern flank.

6:00

"Yes everything's alright." Hannibal said in near perfect Imperial, he then gave a small report to the man on the other side of the communication crystal and ended the conversation.

"Where did you learn Imperial common?" Lance asked him, with a surprised expression on his face.

"There were a couple of Imperial girls in some of the ports I was stationed at, I'll tell you about it some other time, now we need to send a message to our headquarters and sneak back to our own lines." Hannibal said as he surveyed the landscape, trying to find a way out of this.

Excerpt from the diary of Lieutenant Alexander Mackintosh.

It was early morning, and I was trying to eat a kava nut (one of those dome looking spherical piece of fruit that tastes like crap and rotten meat and I was going through a lot of trouble trying to carefully open it, since it had a hard shell with no weak points, and if you're not careful your own strength and tools can hurt or eve cripple yourself) when we received the transmission from Captain Hannibal's extended patrol group about an imminent enemy attack from our Southern Flank.

And since I was the staff officer on duty, it was my job to deliver the message to the commanders of both the Volunian Army and the Republican task force, General Al Hambra and General Pompei.

"I have an urgent message for the commanders, open the doors!" I said to the guards who were stationed outside the high officer's quarters.

"I'm afraid I cannot do that, Lieutenant." one of the guards said to me.

"What! Why not?"

"The generals are having a poker game and have given strict orders to not let anyone disturb them until 12 o clock which is many hours from now." the second guard answered.

"This is more important than a bloody poker game, the enemy is attacking our most vulnerable positions and our army needs orders!" I almost shouted back to the guards, outside you could hear the roar of thunder coming from the sky, echoing across the plains as I waved the message in their faces.

"Let me see that message." the second guard said, and Alexander complied.

Both guards read it and they started debating on whether to disturb them or not, I grew impatient with them, so I took a few steps towards a metal trash can and asked.

"You're orders are that nobody is to intentionally disturb them right?"

"Yes." one of them replied.

And as soon as he said that I started hitting the metal trash can repeatedly and as hard as I could.

"W-What are you doing!?" one of the guards shouted in a panicked voice.

"Why, I am 'unintentionally' creating noise to 'unintentionally' disturb the generals of course!" I said and continued to hit the trash can, which made the occupants of the room open the door to see what was going on.

"Soldier, I better hope you like digging latrines, cause if you don't have a good reason for what you've done, that's what you will be you're duty for the next six months." General Al Hambra the commander of the Volunian infantry said to me.

57

I immediately snatched the message from the guards and gave it to General Pompeii.

As soon as he finished reading it he ripped the note to pieces.

"You disturbed the highest ranking officers of two armies for this nonsense!" General Pompeii our commander said to me with a huff of indignation.

"Nonsense! Sir, the enemy is attacking our rear, they have crossed the forest and our formation is in danger of collapsing!" I said to him, astounded at his reaction.

"Calm yourself Lieutenant, even if they crossed the forest it is just a small diversionary attack at the best, that region is impossible to cross with a real army, it is too rocky and too wooded, the only army that could cross it is fake one meant to fool us, a deception nothing more." the General Pompeii said in a soothing voice as outside the sound of thunder roared.

THUN THUN* THUN* THUN* THUN*

"Exactly! This attack is just a distraction, the main thrust will come from the west where we are strongest, still this is unexpected and you were in the right mind to wake us, give the orders to prepare for an attack from the west." Al Hambra replied.

THUN THUN* THUN* THUN* THUN*

"Sir, what about the supply base!?"

THUN THUN* THUN* THUN* THUN*

"The supply base is guarded by 2.500 men, it has trenches and walls that can stop any diversionary force the enemy has, now get this trough you thick skull the enemy cannot move a proper army trough that wood, the only heavy troops our enemy have are imaginary ones, unless you are afraid of things that go bump in the night!"

THUN THUN* THUN* THUN* THUN*

After Al Hambra's mocking words, everyone else present laughed at my expense.

THUN THUN* THUN* THUN* THUN*

The laughter continued for a few moments until.

*BANG*BOOM* BANG*BOOM* BANG*BOOM*

THUN THUN* THUN* THUN* THUN*

*BANG*BOOM* BANG*BOOM* BANG*BOOM*

THUN THUN* THUN* THUN* THUN*

And following that the laughter the laughter became stuck in their throats.

"W-what was that!?" Pompeii said to those present as they all shocked at what they just heard.

"I believe that was our enemy's imaginary artillery, from their fake army, assaulting our supply base General, but I'm not sure if they go 'bump in the night.'" I replied with a small smile of triumph on my face at the disbelieving looks of the commanders, but that quickly vanished once the grim reality of our current situation sank in and our desperate struggle began.

Lieutenant First Class Alexander Mackintosh, command staff member, Federal Expeditionary force.

Extract from the book "Confessions, an Admirals tale volume I"

There were many things I had done these past few days which are open for debate, I walked about the various installations and positions of the division.

To the common soldier it looked like I was doing a routine inspection, which was expected of the newly minted Commodore of this corps, which I was, but that was not the real reason for my walks.

My main motivation for doing them was to fight off insomnia and as an afterthought I was checking all possible escape routes into the forest and the state of the fuel and ships, so if need be I could desert my command.

The thought of leaving and never coming back, was ever prevalent in my mind, especially since in this age's warfare even a grand admiral is in the same amount of danger as the most worthless foot soldier.

I could have easily taken one of the ships since I was an excellent liar, navigate it to some remote planet, and hide there for the rest of my life, I could have and believe me the great fear I had for the upcoming battle was a great motivator, but I didn't.

Why, you may ask? Well, I am not so sure of the answer myself; perhaps it was that nagging feeling in my head which told me that fleeing in one ship while still within hostile territory was not exactly the brightest idea.

Also it would look odd if the commander was suddenly taking a ships for a 'field test' right before a battle, so I would probably be arrested and court-martialed for trying such, and then sentenced to the firing squad, so certain death if I ran, almost if I stayed. (I guess that is a good enough reason not to desert as any).

Dear God! Sometimes life's very hard for me, though I suspect that it is not true since I have seen other wretches who have it far worse than me and no matter how hard my life gets, one look at them and I feel grateful that even when it gets bad, it could always get worse.

Thus I found myself at the foremost position of our surprise attack, watching our artillery's preliminary bombardment.

Something like this was expected of a sailor of my reputation, the Fox of Marengo, Hero of the Empire or whatever silly name the press calls me now, would always lead from the front!

And it's moments like this I wish I just said kriff you to Commodore Crackerjack, and ran away from him faster than he can say 'here is your commission' all those years ago, but the past is the past and the only thing you get if you linger too much is regret so I suppose I should move on, but that's just my opinion and it's only works for me.

Or so I thought, but if I'd know just what I nightmare being stationed in this particular area of the galaxy would have been at the time I would have done so, and also included in the insult his wife, siblings ,mother, father and kitchenware to boot!"

Metternich per Pelasgiamus, Freelance Potions maker

Metternich with the help of a pair of binoculars surveyed the battle field before him as he stood upright in the backseat of the spider-wolf -jeep with his aide Butz in the driver's seat.

The jeep was a vehicle powered by the very same crystals that fueled the ships. It had instead of wheels circular rings all over the surface of its belly, mimicking the way a snake crawls, which was pretty useful in bad terrain like mud, sand, or even snow.

It's front was as its name suggests shaped like the head of a wolf, this was not only because of a psychological reason, since wolves where creatures which were generally feared, but also a practical reason since sloped and angled armor was more efficient than flat surfaced one at deflecting enemy projectiles, but also to use what was called 'Creed Magic'.

Creed magic at its most basic definition was the simple notion that if you get enough people to believe something no matter how silly or slightly illogical it is, that something can become reality, or at least as close as you can get to reality.

A spider-wolf jeep was made so that when it was viewed by others they thought it was as stealthy and deadly as either a wolf or a snake or a combination of the two, something like this was an advantage since the vehicle was designed to be a scout/anti-infantry weapon.

The same was applied to the other vehicles, from war chariots to ships, to Pegasus, to Titans and even basic armor and swords.

The more deadly it looked the better!

For it was not unheard off for a force which had a superior number of armored units to lose a fight to an opposing one that had fewer heavies, but had such a high mass of infantry that where so convinced that their units where stronger than their foes, that the one's with the fewer heavies actually received a magical bonus from the infantry! Not a big one but enough to tip the scale in their favor and win the day, fight to a draw or at the very least a pyrrhic victory.

The morale of a fighting force could be a decisive factor, since faith and beliefs could be powerful weapons and from the current belief the 378th had, and that they would succeed in their surprise attack, gave them a huge advantage and along with the element of surprise it tipped the scale in their favor. This was evident in the first hour of the battle since they were pushing the enemy back on all fronts.

"A fine starts sir, a fine start indeed!" Adrian said from his position next to Metty's jeep as they gazed at the vanguard of their assault and it was doing a fine job of cutting the enemy to pieces.

In front of them their army was rolling up the enemy nicely, the artillery was doing an exquisite job of pinning down the enemy; the infantry and chariots where pushing them back and the cavalry was breaking their flanks.

"Let's hope we have a good enough ending to this battle as its beginning, tell Tarkan to send half our forces to support the vanguard, the other half we will send as a flanking assault once we engage the enemy, and have Werner and his 88th ready in reserve." Metternich replied.

"Yes sir, also complements of the 12th scouting group, the enemy's cavalry are massing on the left side." Adrian told him, he unlike Metternich was on an armored horse, since he had taken temporary command of the cavalry.

"Excellent!" his commander replied, with a smile on his face.

"And by excellent, I mean nuts and damnation, since it means those bloody monsters are heading this way!"

"You know what to do Adrian, just like Marengo." Metternich said nonchalantly, but inside his stomach was aching and he was close to hyperventilating.

"Do you think it's absolutely necessary sir?" his knight said, his voice filled with worry for his lord.

"I am afraid it is my friend, now begin the maneuver!" Metternich replied.

Adrian gave a reluctant nod, and moved the cavalry far way from where his liege was situated, leaving him with only an escort of about five other spider-wolf jeeps.

He was situated on a small hill about 200 meters in height, which gave him a clear view of the battlefield.

Metternich stole a gaze towards his side and saw that the flag of the commander was being raised next to him.

As he looked towards the enemy he saw that they were preparing to charge.

Apparently the sight of the enemy's commander guarded by only a handful of troops and no Imperial cavalry in sight was to great temptation to pass up.

"I could still run, defect, I could order Butz to withdraw..........No!.....Not here...............And not now, it's too dangerous! The jeep would eventually run out of fuel and if these troops see me run, the whole damn front would collapse!" Metternich bitterly thought to himself, as enemy arrows and lances were thrown from a distance at his position from the skirmish fraction of the enemy cavalry.

"I guess it's time to get started, Butz retire the Guard behind the crest and give the order to prepare for phase one." he said to his aide.

"Yes sir!" his aide replied and moved the jeep and its escort behind the crest of the hill.

"They come at us in the same old style." Metternich said to his aide.

"Then we will just have to receive them in the same in style." Butz replied with a smile on his face.

Excerpt from the memoires of Private Raz V'a van;

"We were the legionaries of Malus, the World Breaker"

I witnessed the portion of the battlefield where Metternich was positioned and what happened next was typical of the chaotic nature of war, the Commander was seemingly isolated and the enemy cavalry charged en masse after firing a few skirmish shots at him.

A cavalry charge was a truly devastating sight to behold, those who had fire or air weapons pointed their swords and spears forwards, turning themselves into a either a blazing fireball or a miniature hurricane, the ones who had water made a small pond around their horse and used that to create a veritable tidal wave out of their respective charges, one that was designed to break their foes and finally the earth side of them did the same as the water creating what can only be described as a miniature landslides, and a uphill one at that!

It was a terrifying sight, a flood, an avalanche, a hurricane, and a small volcano eruption all headed for our commander. But as they got to the crest of the hill all of a sudden explosions rattled them, I realized then that our small supply of mines that were too few to make a decent defensive perimeter had all been placed on that small hilltop, turning what was insignificant to the battle into the decisive factor!

As the enemy cavalry unknowingly stepped towards their doom, fire, water and air exploded from the ground beneath them breaking their charge, the troops at the very front were dead, the middle ones where wounded and the rear guard of the charge was tripping over their forward comrades.

And when those poor souls in the enemy cavalry thought it was over the earth mines sprang to life, forming battle Golems and upon taking the shapes of various beast and monster from mythology and some from your nightmares they started attacking and decimating them.

But these were not green troops, war had barely arrived to this portion of the galaxy, so these where still professional soldiers, they regained their senses, regrouped and started to reorganize themselves and push back the Golems.

As things seemed to be becoming bleak for the commander, a sudden trumpet bugle was heard and I witnessed some of the rear units of the cavalry turning their heads to see what was going on, they had only a few moments to see the Imperial cavalry lead by Commodore de Morowetz doing a counter *charge on their rear, which plowed through them like hot knife through butter, those that were at the front of the formation tried one last desperate charge trough the Golems in the faint hopes of reaching Metternich, but their effort was for naught, for right behind the crest of the hill, was the 88th which greeted the enemy cavalry with blood and iron, our iron their blood."*

Private Raz V'a van; Imperial Engineers Corps

Adrian hacked and slashed his way through the enemy cavalry, cutting fire swords, water axes, air spears and earth maces and flails, after a few moments of the combinations of being trapped by the mines and being flanked by the Imperial forces, the Volunian cavalry broke and ran, only to be chased by the Imperial cavalry and for what was left of it to be cut to pieces.

7:03 Local time

"My lord, are you alright?!?" Adrian asked him as he looked at Metternich who was holding a wounded soldier upwards, with one of the soldier's hands over his shoulder.

"Fine and dandy, but our friend here requires medical attention, also Adrian I want you to give the orders to get the reserves ready to advance as soon as Tarkan requests it, Butz I want word of Valyria's situation, tell her not to overdo it, if she can just prevent the enemy on the hills from reinforcing the rear then that's enough, she doesn't have to take the heights." The Commander of the fleet replied as he handed the wounded soldier to an ambulance squad.

"Yes sir!" Butz and Adrian replied as they went to carry their duties.

Metternich gave a quick look around him, as the faces of the soldiers who had up until now where filled a mixture of hope with apprehension, uncertainty and sometimes downright contempt and hatred for their new commander where filled with respect, awe and the beginning of loyalty and dedication.

So he gave them all a genuine smile before returning to his jeep, it never hurt to be liked by others.

7:03

Valyria watched from her vantage point as her troops demonstrated against the enemy stationed on the hills.

For now everything seemed to be going smoothly, so far her troops were in a heavy skirmish with the Volunians. It was a fight that could be maintained for a long period of time, despite the fact that the enemy before her had a more elevated position and greater numbers.

She achieved this by moving her units to the foot of the hill, where it was so abruptly angled that the enemy could not lower their artillery enough to shoot a decent barrage on them.

This allowed her to maintain her front and actually give her smaller attacking force an advantage over the larger and better positioned enemy units.

"All seems to be going well." she muttered underneath her breath.

"Ma'am, major Evans is reporting that the enemy is intensifying its barrage on her flank." one of her aide said.

"The enemy is starting to organize its defenses, have all of our earth breakers fire on the enemies right flank, then move to the center, then towards Evans on the left, then back right and so one. That will confuse the enemy, making them think we have a much stronger forces than what we really have and take the pressure of Evans."

"Also order the following: the forces that we have in reserve will begin an extended patrol to deceive the enemy of our true strength and position, fire, disengage, redeploy and fire once more, that should confuse them." Valyria sad to her aide and he quickly send the orders down the line.

As she continued to receive dispatches and give orders to her subordinates her mind flashed back to the very beginning of this operation.

****

"I have never seen something like this before, using our ships as giant bulldozers and the uprooted trees as a road is such an absurd idea!" Valyria said to Tarkan.

"Perhaps, but so is our current situation, also when you think about it, all we really needed to clear a path through the woods was something big and heavy enough to plow through it, we never really thought about this, since we see the ships as tools of war, not construction equipment." Tarkan replied to her.

"That's not a very funny joke Tarkan." she said to him.

"What do you mean?" He asked and raised an inquisitive eyebrow.

"Everyone thought of an idea like this, but no one voiced it, since no one wanted to risk losing what little we had left and be the one to blame if things went from bad to worse." she replied.

"And what grounds do you have for such a conclusion?" he asked her, an amused smile on his face.

"You're absolutely right, I have no grounds for it, it's not like I went to school with most of you and had known and fought alongside you all for years, no sir! I have nothing that would give me the necessary means of reading my colleagues thoughts!" she replied and tried to stiff a laugh on her insect like features.

"Couldn't have said it better myself!" Tarkan replied with a chuckle, to which Valyria gave in and indulged in a brief one herself.

"Anyway let's hope this all goes well, I'm dressed for victory not defeat." she said.

"That is not a problem for me." Tarkan said with a smile.

At this Valyria raised a confused eyebrow at Tarkan, daring him to elaborate, at which he replied with a smile on his face.

"My wardrobe has clothes for both disasters and blessings." he said and what followed was a moment of silence, during which Valyria looked at him with a surprised expression, before finally giving in and laughing out loud. Tarkan joined her as well and their laughter helped defuse if only temporary their trepidations for the upcoming battle.

* *

She lowered her field binoculars as a smile appeared on her face as the flashback ended.

"You do actually have exquisite taste Tarkan and a beautiful wardrobe, please be safe my friend and come back alive, I do not want you to earn your place in the Hall of Heroes in this Force of Creation forsaken place!" she thought to herself.

378th corps flanking force, Tarkan's position.

7:08

Tarkan looked at his division as it was pushing back the enemy and saying that he was happy was an understatement if there ever was one, things were going well and with reports coming in that the enemy cavalry was routed and destroyed, the situation seemed to be getting better and better.

"This is Commodore Tarkan calling in, we have identified the locations of the enemies rear units, we are ready for phase two, repeat ready for phase two, I am requesting support the from 88th." he transmitted to his commander and used his binoculars to more once more observe the battle.

"A fine pattern we are weaving here today, a fine one indeed!"

**Excerpt from the diary of Lieutenant Alexander Mackintosh.**

Despite my more than unconventional and borderline on insubordination 'report' the commanders where far too busy trying to get a grasp of the situation to deal with me, or at least for now they were too busy to deal with me.

"Move units from the hills and towards the supply base, if we can hold it then we can repulse the enemy. Tell the commanders on the hills to launch a full scale offensive, since the enemy before them is only a delaying force." General Al Hambra said to his subordinates.

General Pompeii was giving orders to our own forces to pull out of the frontlines and send troops towards the supply dump to support our counterattack, when I received another message from our forces there.

"General! Major Dantuine reports that his forces have been nearly pushed out of the supply base, the enemy has overrun almost three fourths of it!" I said to the general.

"Transmit that information to the troops, also let them know that three months worth of food rations are in that base, that should motivate them to get it back." he replied and I could see the logic in that, I just hoped it worked.

Lieutenant First Class Alexander Mackintosh, command staff member, Federal Expeditionary force.

The forces of the Federation were being beaten back on all fronts from the supply base and the mixed force of infantry and navy personal were all too happy to pursue them.

As they were pushed back, the Federals noticed a shadow behind them, the retreating forces looked at it and saw the hand of God, or rather one of his servants in the form of a priest.

"Evil is amongst us! Stand back, this calls for divine intervention!" The priest said and ran in front of the nearest Imperial squadron.

The first soldier charged with his flame sword and slashed at the priest; he sidestepped, grabbed the soldier's hand with his right arm and then gave a powerful jab with his left, one that shattered the soldier's arm at his elbow joint.

He then ducked out of the way of another one's water lance attack and gave a powerful sweeping kick which hit the second soldier's knee cap; the third soldier fired an air arrow at the priest and a fourth one took out his earth mace, activating the magic within it.

The mace's metal began to rotate and oscillate into a deadly spherical chainsaw-like pattern.

The priest simply caught the arrow and threw it back at the third soldier, impaling his bow drawing hand while side stepping the fourth soldier's mace, tripping him and as he fell down the priest gave a powerful kick in the soldier's side, shattering his ribs.

"He's a monster!" one of the Imperials shouted, as he witnessed four of his comrades being taken down effortlessly.

"No I'm not, name's Alexander Turneissnen Herman Eist, but my congregation calms me A.T.H for short; and I kick ass for the lord!" The priest shouted to those gathered and the remaining Imperials quickly retreated back to their main group, giving the federals some respite.

"Wait, you're nickname is A.T.H?" one federal soldier asked.

"Yes!"

"And you're family name is Eist?"

"Yes, of course!"

"So you're A.T.H Eist, the priest!?!"

"Yes, I know! But my parents gave me the name and I love my parents, so just call me Turneissnen!" he told them.

After talking with them and making sure they where alright Turneissnen turned towards the direction of the enemy; he took what looked like one big club from his belt and pointed it towards the Imperials.

"Now then, the people in front of us are heathens and it's our holy duty to preach the word of God to them, so let us go and spread the gospel!" he said to the assembled troopers who rallied behind him as he led a counter-attack on the Imperial assault.

378ᵗʰ corps, Metternich's command position.

8:23 Local time.

As he observed the battle before him, his comm crystal shimmed indicating that he had a new message.

"Yes, what is it?"

"Sir, complements of Commodore Jackson, we have our report on the Federal Forces there."

"Well go on man, people are shooting at me!" he thought to himself as everywhere around him the battle raged on with fire and sword.

"Sir, from enemy prisoners and our own scouts, we've discovered that the Holy Knights stationed here have been recalled back to Galiana, apparently yesterday was their last tour of duty and they've been rotated from the frontlines with a fresh new battalion of non Holy Knights!" the communications officer replied, his voice barely able to contain his enthusiasm.

"T-this means that this planet is now beret of Holy Knights!"

"I want that transmission to be broadcasted to every soldier and sailor we have with us, let them know we have the advantage and tell them to press it home!" he ordered.

"YES SIR!!!!"

After that Metternich returned his gaze to the battlefield, and what he saw dampened his spirit a little bit.

"Looks like the enemy is starting to push us back." The young commodore thought to himself as he observed the battle.

"Butz, tell Werner that it's his turn, he is to take his Brigade and stop the enemy counterattack." Metternich told his aide.

"Yes sir!" Butz replied and relayed the orders trough the communications crystal attached to their jeep's windwaker.

"Things are going ok for now, if we can break through here, smash the last of the supply guards and capture enough fresh crystals we can withdraw from this rock!" Metternich thought to himself as he gaze a glance to his rear where the 88th was kept in reserve.

Its commanders had protested against this, with Werner being the exception, a fact that surprised the others, but Metternich assured them that when the enemy would send in their reinforcements they would be the decisive factor, now he hoped that they lived to up to their reputation, for in their current state he doubted that they could carry the day in a battle of attrition, they had to finish this soon!

So he hoped that the 88th would be enough to hold the lines long enough for him to play his final card.

Extract from the diary of Corporal D'hrain Jeran.

In a battle, the strength and weaknesses of the each element went like this:

Fire beats air, air beats earth, earth beats water and water beats fire; situations outside of that like water fighting earth and wind fighting water or fire against earth depend more on the warriors wielding them, but the aforementioned strengths and weaknesses is generally how you want to use your troops in an orderly manner.

But during that black morning on Volunia 4 there was no order of battle, only one big schoolyard brawl.

The day had started with a rather lovely early morning darkness, but as the minutes went by, clouds gathered over the hot plain we were all stationed.

When the first bolt of lightning was heard in the distance our officers told us to relax and stand down, since it was unlikely that the enemy to attack during a thunderstorm, after all your fist instinct when a storm starts is to get inside as quick as you can and wait for it to pass, which was good and sound advice and we where fools for listening to it that day!

The thunderstorm booming in the distance was raging out so loud that it helped mask the enemies movements and eventual attack, what made matters even worse was the fact that by the time the attack had commenced the storm not only had intensified, but had also reached our position as well.

For the first few minutes of the attack you could not have guessed we had been ambushed do to the weather, but when you saw a squad of infantrymen, followed by a company and then a battalion all running as fast as they could away from the rear position it was clear what was happening.

So my battalion quickly formed up for battle and took up a position to face the enemy, our regimental Colonel was yelling, shouting and sometimes even shooting at our comrades to get them to rally behind us to meet the enemy.

And it was starting to work, as more and more soldiers began to join our ranks and started to form up, but by then it was too late; I somehow managed to survive that day and also stay alive long enough to get a discharge from the army and get back home and spend the rest of the war safe, and although I fought 20 more battle after that, each of them more fiercer than Volun 4, but I will never forget what I saw during the first few hours of the battle.

The enemy had attacked with such speed and ferocity that any manner of formation or discipline was lost, only raw power and momentum was used for their attacks.

Normally that's not what you do in a battle, but at that point it didn't matter, they had ambushed us so fast and in so great numbers that it was impossible to get any formation up, and those that did where quickly swallowed whole by the Imperial tidal wave.

I saw ranks of air soldiers shot at by so many earth warriors that the formation was reduced to nothing but a pile or ruble and mangled flesh, I saw whole companies of fire troopers hit so hard and in so great numbers by water soldiers that they hardly stood a chance, and when they finely got to us they where a mixture of fire, water, earth and wind, a nightmare to any commander to try and lead, but that did not matter, the image of so many of our own troops being cut down and breaking ranks greatly boosted the enemy's morale and subsequent Creed Magic.

Thus we saw and felt its effects, their fire blazed like an inferno, the wind and water attacks grew in size and shape into vortexes around their weapons, that spun so fast they could cut through our ranks like they were paper, the earth troops weapons grew so much in size and sharpness that they seemed more like the claws and teeth of some ancient monster, than that of mere mortals.

As what lay before us closed in for the kill, we all felt that we where now hopelessly outmatched and even before the enemy reached our line I saw men break ranks, making our formation becoming even thinner.

And as the enemy struck us, a whole wall of men and weaponry and least 50 long and ten ranks deep was pushed back!

Somehow we did not break at contact, but as they continued to push, we felt the ground beneath our feet running away from us as the whole column was pushed back; 'everything was lost and nothing short of divine intervention could save us' was the thought going through my head as our formation was starting to fall apart and from one of the gaps the enemy poured trough, but just as that happened a figure ran past me and straight into that herd of xenos monsters and divine help had arrived in the not so surprising form of a priest.

Corporal D'hrain Jeran.

Volunian army.

"The Almighty God Jasee is mercy and love incarnate, feel his love!" the short trimmed blond haired, glasses wearing face of Turneissnen gave this as a battle cry while the priest hit and bashed his way through the Imperial ranks, stemming the tide.

The mighty repeated blows of his weapon not only slayed those before him, but the Imperials where so tightly packed from the charge that the sheer kinetic force unleashed by the club affected the ones that were too close to the attacked soldiers.

With such a ferocious counter-attack Alexander had not only stopped the Imperials from exploiting the gap in the Federal lines, he was also pushing them back!

Behind him the Federal troops upon seeing this quickly rallied on his person and plugged the gap making the Federal formation whole again.

As Turneissnen slashed, parried, weaved and dodged trough his opponents, the whole section he was fighting was actually beginning to fall back.

"All units push forward, the charge is broken! Push them back!" the priest bellowed out to his allies as he continued to cut his way through the enemy.

At this the whole flow of the battle changed as Federal fire warriors blazed away, earth warriors shifted the surface of their shields to form spike shieldwalls, that started to spin and move along its surface turning the formation into a shieldwall of humming chainsaw teeth.

Air troops followed and launched arrows and spears engulfed in miniature vortexes that made them move too fast for the common eye to see, and finally the aqua warriors of the Federation joined in with their spears and maces, their weapons contained water and they made it flow in a pattern all across their weapon's surface with such a strong flow, that the water turned solid and moved fast enough to cut almost anything in its path.

They surged forward, extending the reach and flow of their water weapons until they could strike not only the ranks in front of them, but also the second rank behind the first and even the third rank as well.

"Oh, you poor xenos heathens, did you actually think you could stand against a holy priest? But don't be sad, for it is not your fault, you are merely ignorant of the error of your ways! After we win, I will be more than happy to open your eyes and convert you to the proper gospel!" the priest shouted as he lashed out and charged the nearest gathering of Imperial troops, who were on the verge of routing.

Nothing seemed to stop him, he dodged the swift air arrows, sidestepped the long reaching water spears, deflected the blazing inferno that was the fire warriors and smashed through any stalwart earth warrior that faced him.

"Flee heathens! The forces of heaven will never be beaten when they fight for their own soil!" Turneissnen bellowed out again, as dust and a cloud of smoke from the fighting began to cover the field, he charged once more, and raised his arm to give another blow at the Imperials, when much to his surprise a fire axe appeared, seemingly out of nowhere and blocked his attack with so much strength that he was forced to jump a foot backwards to ride the force of the blow.

9:36 Local Planetary time

"Sorry priest, but you may call the shots in your version of heaven, but you're too far away from home for that." the shape of an Imperial Officer came out of the dust cloud.

"This isn't heaven, it's hell and here you don't rule, I DO!" the officer added and charged Turneissnen.

A fury of blows, thrusts and parries followed, all of which seemed to fast to be anything less than either two divine or two cursed being clashing blades.

After a few minutes of relentless fighting, the two opponents broke off their attacks and both of them took two steps backwards to catch their breath.

"What is your name and which unit do you belong heathen? You do not look like the rest!" Turneissnen said as he took a few deep breath of air to quench the fire in his lungs.

"Black Beret Corps, 88th brigade, you'll know us as the kriffing sons and daughters of towngirls that's going to send your pathetic excuse for soldiers to hell! As for the name, it's Colonel Werner von Braun!" he replied.

"That would be quite a feat for you, considering you're units will be doing it without their heads!" Turneissnen replied to Werner's taunt.

At this the Federal troops were unnerved as they realized that a member of the deadly Black Berets was their new opponent, what was even more alarming was the fact that as the dust began to settle, they could see that behind Werner, there were troops who on their arms had the seal of a sword in flames and that each helmet contained a black plumage feather.

The rest of the Black Berets had arrived on the field!

"Hellfires, ey? Ha! You're reputation precedes you and I see it is well merited!" Turneissnen said as he maneuvered the club to his back and jammed it inside what appeared to be the orifice of a very large shield; he then pulled the club with one arm, with the shield now attached to it, revealing that it was in fact a great earth sword and that the club was its handle.

His body armor then overflowed with magic as he summoned his battle aura and extracted a huge amount of power from his energy crystals which he had on himself and filled his sword with raw energy.

The edges of the earth sword grew teeth and they started moving rapidly across it surface making into a massive chain blade, it moved so fast that the teeth turned red and it made a buzzing sound of almost hellish nature.

"Time to stop this warm up and get serious wouldn't you agree?" the priest challenged him.

"I agree." Werner said with a smile on his face and his fire axe whose flames already blazed like a furnace suddenly became a body of fire so intense that it looked like a small piece of the sun was what Werner was wielding, and with these great weapons the battle of two titans resumed.

The occupied Territories, Maramanakama.

The party had been going on for a few hours and it was still a jolly time in Ahmaiano's apartment and considering that the apartment was small, overcrowded with people and thanks to their recent actions against the empire, smelling along with the rest of the street like a latrine that was no small accomplishment!

"Can I talk with you for a second?" Tubarin said to Ahmaianos, at which he nodded and they both went to a secluded corner, away from the party.

"What is it?" Ahmaianos asked.

"I say we get as far away as we can from that 'Nobody' clown."

"What do you mean, didn't he helped us?"

"Oh, come on Ahmaianos, can't you smell just how fowl the whole thing actually is?"

"Well, the sewer pipe we blew up is making things rather intolerable."

"Not that! I mean what happened today, you know everything is hunky dory, until Mr Trouble comes in to town, and he starts making everything unbearable and no matter what you do you can't stop him, until finally you scream for all the world to hear ' I'll do anything, follow anyone, juts please help me!'"

"And then Mr Salvation comes along, and he ask you for this and that and you give him want he wants and more because he stops Mr Trouble, but what you don't know is that after the whole thing is over and their not in public Mr Trouble and Mr Salvation turn out to be friends and split what they earned fifty-fifty." Tubarin told him.

At this Ahmaianos was silent for a moment while he contemplated his answer before replying with:

"It may very well be a sting operation, I wouldn't put it past the Empire to be this sadistic, but I'll be honest with you, there might be a chance that it's a genuine anti-Imperial group that we had just had contact with, we should be cautious about this, but not all together dismissive."

"All right, but I still think it's too good to be true, though I'm surprise you're this opened minded!"

"Well, I know a lot about scams and cons, half of my neighbors from before the war where the best con artists and thieves in Tolina." Ahmaianos told him.

"What! Who the hell did you live next door to?"

"Guess."

"Mafia dons, loan sharks and smugglers?"

"Lawyers and stock brokers."

At this, they both shared a laugh which helped to lighten the mood between them.

"Have you shared your thoughts with any of the others?" Ahmaianos whispered to him as they look at the other members of their small group who were still celebrating.

"Nah, I may be a jerk but I'm not a big enough jerk to spoil a party, maybe I'll run it by them tomorrow after they sober up. Besides, we've lost so much in these past few years, our country, our pride, our livelihoods, our friends, so much so that we barely have any reason to be happy, so any excuse for a party, even a stupid one is good enough to shut me up!" Tubarin replied with a smile.

"I'll remember that!" Ahmaianos teased him, and Tubarin playfully punched him in the chest and they shared another laugh before returning to the party.

"We were the legionaries of Malus, The World Breaker"

About two days before the battle, I managed to find a small pub within a nearby trading post and on this uncolonised planet it was the only civilian settlements you could find, it's name was quaintly called the WestCoast, the place seemed to be ok with serving Imperial troops, but in regards to their hospitality I suspect that the big pieces of sharpened steel we carried with us played an important factor.

I sat there for a few hours, ordering local cuisine until I noticed that it was time to return to the battalion, I was about to get up and join the rest when a certain biological need compelled me to visit the bathroom, so I ventured towards the higher levels of the pub and after finding the restroom and sitting on the toiled in order to relieve my need, I saw that to the wall of the stall I was using there was some kind of talisman or totem attached to it.

I'm not sure what it was called or what it even was, but it looked appealing so I extended my arm to touch it, and as I did so a strange and not altogether unpleasant sensation washed over me.

I quickly removed my hand, and could have just ignored the totem there and then, but curiosity got the better of me so I touched it again.

I closed my eyes for a few moments and when I opened them what I saw before myself was beyond description, colors flashed and faded, matter appeared and disappeared, before me there was a great void which appeared to be infinity itself, and a great mass which seemed thicker than the black eternity of space, and more thin than the spring sunlight of the most sacred planet.

But the most strangest and indescribable thing of all was that the sight before me seemed not to change or even remain constant, what it was I could not guess, all I know that it was something I was not suppose to see.

"It is existence." a voice said behind me, I wanted to look around and see who did it belong to, but I decided to get my bearings straight first.

"Existence? Why is it here, why am I hear, why me and who are you?" I asked it.

"It was never just here, it's everywhere, this moment and this place is one of the few instances when you can see it. As for you, I'd say that you are here but because you chose this." the voice replied.

"I....I chose this?"

"Yes."

"What the hell does that mean?"

"Well don't ask me, I can't explain it and I don't have time to!"

76

"Wait! How did you get here, who and what are you?"

"My name is Icarius Reign, as to how I got here; well I'll give you an answer when I find one, until then bye!" the voice replied and that was the last I heard of it.

With its absence, the sheer incomprehensibility of this place started to get to me.

I closed my eyes, pressed the palm of my hands to the side of my head in an attempt to block out both the pure madness and untainted sanity which resided in that place, I screamed to the heavens for release and I received it.

As I opened my eyes, I saw that I had returned to the bathroom and after a few long breaths to calm myself I walked out of the stool and left the pub, there where eyes upon me, with various reactions to what happened in the bathroom or what they thought happened .

What really went on that day I am not completely sure , maybe it was real, maybe it was caused by the stress for the upcoming battle, maybe that amulet was some weird drug, maybe it was me finally cracking up, or maybe it was that meal I had, for at that point in my life, I was not aware of the significance of the name Icarius, but thrust me, that name would one day be on everybody's lips!

Private Raz V'a van; Imperial Engineers Corps

9:36

"The beginning, a most wondrous time for almost anybody and everybody." Deux who was high above the mortal plane of existence started scribing away what he just witnessed.

Down below the faces of Metternich's new immediate subordinates where al cheerful and happy as the battle was seemingly going their way.

"To many people, the beginning is the start of something new and exciting."

Alexander and Werner where still clashing blades, each giving the other his best attack, both expecting that after this blow the final strike would come, but neither one of them was able to outmatch the other, much to their frustration, and warrior's joy.

"To others it is something unexpected."

The various Maramanakaman rebels or terrorist where all watching the news with surprise at what happened today. The Local Imperial administration had tried to censor it, but the power of the press somehow got trough, and amongst the rebels, in a hidden base on a certain moon, there was a former soldier now resistance fighter called Alefran who was watching the latest news with great interest.

"To some it could be their greatest wish finally coming true."

Kalynka had taken the communication crystal which the voice of Nobody was heard from and was looking at it intensely, she did not know what the future would bring, but was certain that it was far better than the past or the present, that thought made a smile on grace her lips.

"To others the beginning brings great challenges and hardships."

Hannibal and Lance where both sneaking their squad around the enemy infantry, trying and for now succeeding at avoiding the Imperial army on their long journey back to safety, but the morning light had arrived, the Imperials where many, and the thunder storm was very deadly.

"To a few it means great disappointments and failures."

Gelios was now by himself and drowning his sorrow with various strong spirits; this day had been a disaster! How much prestige did he lose? How many terrorists would be emboldened by this? How could something that originally seemed like a cakewalk become such an embarrassment and also what he could do to salvage the situation?

"To others, it brings great dangers."

Metternich looked towards the direction of the enemy knowing that it was not over, the battle was still in the balance and even if they won, tomorrow there would be another battle, followed by another fight the next day, and another one after that.

He closed his eyes in the vain hope that this horrid nightmare would be over and he would wake up and go to work tomorrow brewing potions as usual, instead of dodging death each day.

"To others the beginning is simply a repeat of what has happened before."

Adrian smiled as he watched what was happening all around the battlefield.

It was just like Marengo and the many countless battles both in space and land that preceded it, a risky plan that resulted in a hopeless situation turning into an astonishing victory!

And he expected no less from his liege Metternich!

"No more hiding, no more running away! Do you hear me enemies of the Empire, this is the beginning of our counterattack!"

"But regardless of what the beginning is for its participants one thing is certain and that for better or worse, regardless of whatever horrors or wonders it brings, and despite what measure of joy and sorrow it creates, the beginning would always be the start of a journey where every beginning is a new ending and every ending is a new beginning."

Deux finished writing in his book, flipped the page and with his ink feather in his hand, he was ready to write the next chapter and all that it entails too, as bellow him the sands of time marched on as one chapter ended and a new one was about to begin.

"Turn back now; less all nightmares know your name!"

Old sailors proverb.

www.ingramcontent.com/pod-product-compliance
Lightning Source LLC
Chambersburg PA
CBHW070536130626
46555CB00003B/1446